Not Over You

A Healing Springs Novel

Amanda Torrey

Not Over You
A Healing Springs Novel
Amanda Torrey

Copyright 2014 Amanda Torrey

All rights reserved. This book or any portion thereof may not be reproduced or used in any manner whatsoever without the express written permission of the publisher except for the use of brief quotations in a book review.
This book is a work of fiction. Any references to historical events, real people, or real locales are used fictitiously. Other names, characters, places, and incidents are the product of the author's imagination, and any resemblance to real persons, living or dead, is entirely coincidental.

www.AmandaTorrey.com

Dedicated to

My loyal readers.
Writing is a solitary business, but knowing that someone is reading these books keeps me going.
Thank you for being the best readers out there.

Chapter One

Everywhere she looked, Savannah was reminded of the painful reality that ten years ago, nearly to the day, she had killed her baby brother.

She adjusted her car's visor to block the blinding sun as she slowed to a crawl in the school zone. The old maple tree in the school yard still stood proudly, shading the giant sandbox. The row of swings continued to move as if children had jumped off seconds before, yet the playground was vacant and lonely.

They were probably evacuated and on lock down when word spread about Savannah Grace coming back to town.

She cranked her music up louder. Her radio choices were limited here in Healing Springs, and even the angriest heavy metal couldn't drown the horror of a haunting memory.

Sensing her anxiety, Rocco, her formerly stray Rottweiler/now pampered wannabe lapdog, nuzzled her neck from his position in the back seat. She stroked his head, tempted to pull over and take him for a run here and now.

"You wanna run, my prince? I'm sorry—I know you prefer to be called 'my warrior.' Oh, you like that, huh?" She scratched his neck with her free hand as she navigated the slightly curvy road that lead to the center of town. She remembered the route to her parent's house as if it had been etched into her brain; her own personal mapping system. She knew the shortcuts and carefully avoided them.

She chanced a look at her cell, annoyed—and yes, ashamed—to see the five missed calls from her stepfather. True, she had said she'd leave first thing this morning and she should have arrived hours earlier. Did he have any idea how easy procrastinating could be when forced to emerge from exile?

A giant sign on the side of the road caught her attention with its gold block lettering etched into polished wood. "Healing Springs. Repairing Broken Spirits Since 1836."

Well that was new. And deceptive.

Rocco's bark startled her, making her jump in her seat and hit her head on the visor. "Ouch. What the heck was that fo—"

Her airbags deployed as she crashed into the truck in front of her. As the powder settled, panic stopped the flow of blood to her extremities. She frantically called out for her dog.

"Rocco, are you okay?" She unbuckled her seatbelt and maneuvered so she could see in the back seat. Rocco struggled to pick himself up off the floor. At her call, he pawed his way up to lick her face.

Knowing he was okay, she reached for her door

handle. She wasn't the praying type, but she fervently mumbled a prayer that the people in the truck were okay. When the door wouldn't open, she moved in her seat so she could kick it with both feet.

Before she could kick, the door flew open. A man in what appeared to be an EMT uniform stood in front of her, reaching a hand out to help her get up.

She ignored his hand and stood, telling Rocco to stay. "You guys work fast. I just crashed a second ago. I'm okay, but we need to check the truck I hit."

"No need to worry. It was me." A smile tickled his voice, and a shiver ran down her back.

That voice was familiar. It ran through her nightmares every single night.

It couldn't be.

She closed her eyes and channeled her DVD yoga instructor. *Deep, cleansing breaths.*

"You've got a little blood on your face. Let me take a look."

"Don't touch me," she snapped as he came close to touching her cheek. Rocco growled, jumping to the front seat. She raised her hand in Rocco's direction to settle him. "I meant to say, 'I'm okay.'"

"Savannah."

He knew who she was.

She brushed the blood off her cheek as she finally dared to look into his face.

He was older, his looks more rugged and with more facial hair than he had at nineteen, but he was the same Quentin Elliot she had loved in high school.

"I'm sorry I hit you. Let me grab my insurance information."

"My truck is fine. But you won't be able to drive this thing."

Rocco whined, and Savannah was grateful for the distraction. "Need to go potty?"

"Potty?" Quentin laughed.

She shot him a warning look, then turned back to the dog. "Come on, my warrior."

Rocco leapt from the car at Savannah's call. She smiled when she noticed Quentin backing up ever-so-slightly. Was he afraid of her sweet dog? Most people were—something about the breed tended to put people off-balance. Worked for her—what better way to ward off unwanted attention?

"There's a leash law..." Quentin began.

"He's fine—he listens better than most people." Rocco hurried to the sidewalk and found a tree to relieve himself on, then trotted back. He stood next to Savannah and nudged his head against her leg. She reached down to scratch his ear.

"Anyway, I guess I should move this to the side and call for a tow. Don't want to keep you from doing whatever you're doing." She turned her back to Quentin, more for her own self-protection than for any sense that she actually had to take action on the vehicle.

"Savannah, I'm glad you're back."

"Thanks, but it won't be for long."

"I had heard you might be coming, but Rick wasn't sure you'd actually make it."

Not Over You

"What's that supposed to mean?" Savannah glared at him, but she knew exactly what was meant. She was unreliable. Not the sort you'd want to pin your high hopes on. Even Rick, the man who had raised her as his own daughter since she was two, doubted her ability to follow through on her promise.

"Calm down, Peaches." She shivered at his use of the nickname he teased her with in high school. "He said you weren't able to commit. Something about work, I think."

"Yeah, well, this isn't exactly something I could refuse, is it?" She shook her head and pursed her lips as she turned her attention to the one highlight of her life—her dog.

"It's still nice that you're doing it. No one expected it, you know."

"Well she is my mother. Why she'd want any part of me—even my bone marrow—is beyond me."

"Savannah, you have to know that she—"

"Don't go there, Quentin." She refused to rehash or relive or in any way dissect her past, present, or future. She was here with the hopes that she would be a suitable match for her mother. Since she had been responsible for the death of the woman's child, saving her life in some small way was the least she could offer.

"Come on, I'll give you a lift."

He pulled her duffel bag out of the back seat, swinging it over his shoulder effortlessly. She appreciated the way his biceps tensed and bunched.

"Anything in your trunk?"

She jerked her eyes away from his musculature, praying her blush didn't show. She faked a cough. "No, that's it."

"You travel light." His brown eyes freaking *twinkled*, melting her like a chocolate bar in the heat.

"Like I told you, I'm not staying long. And I can't accept a ride from you. Thanks anyway."

He looked past her, leaving her wondering what he was thinking.

"Ah, the town welcome committee has arrived. They'll be thrilled to welcome you back to town with open arms."

Crap. Just what she didn't need. This town suffocated. The people in it wouldn't know an emotional boundary if you drew it in their own blood.

"Actually, I'll take that ride after all. If the offer still stands."

He had the audacity to laugh as he tossed her bag in the passenger compartment of his extended cab truck. Rocco followed her to the truck, which he jumped into with no trouble.

"Man, your dog takes up a lot of space."

"He's a big dog." She nuzzled Rocco's neck, desperately trying to hide her face from the group of Healing Springs townies who were quickly approaching the street.

"Be right back, I have to turn your hazards on."

"Please hurry."

Quentin swung into the driver's seat and started the truck seconds before the townies made it to Savannah. He waved with great enthusiasm as they drove away. She could only imagine the disappointed looks on the intruding faces.

"They move fast." Savannah shuddered, grateful for the escape.

"Yeah, even good old Bruce with his walker."

"He's still around?"

"I think he secretly died decades ago, but refuses to stop haunting the town."

Savannah sobered at the mention of death. He must have noticed her abrupt withdrawal, because she could feel him glance at her as she looked out the window. His arm reached across to touch her knee, but Rocco's warning growl made him pull away just as his fingertips grazed her skin.

"I'll take care of your car after I drop you off."

She couldn't reply at first. But then she remembered her manners and the fact that she had hit his vehicle and he was stuck coming to her rescue. She did what she did best—she buried her feelings and put on a mask.

"At this point I don't even care what happens to it. Does Harvey still collect things in his yard? Maybe he can keep it for a lawn ornament. I'm sure his neighbors would appreciate that."

He laughed, and she had to fight to keep her expression neutral.

"It would certainly make for a lively 'Letters to the Editor' page."

Savannah tuned out of the conversation to focus on the road ahead. Her insides twisted and her palms sweat at the imminent doom that faced her around the next corner—they'd soon be pulling into her parent's driveway.

Quentin probably didn't realize that his presence actually helped calm her fiery nerves. She'd never admit it.

Over the years, Savannah had struggled to keep the memory of anything good buried deep in whatever was left of her soul. Quentin fit firmly into that category. He had always brought out the best in her, except that day when he was an accomplice in her brother's death.

The silence could have been more awkward if it hadn't been for Rocco's excitement giving her the distraction she needed. Rather than attempting small talk, Savannah gave all of her attention to her animal companion, vowing to force a manicure on him as he dug his nails into her thighs while trying to get a good look out the window. She supposed it was worse for Quentin—he got the tail end of the pooch.

At the first view of her parent's house, she considered begging Quentin to take her anywhere but there. But her phone was lighting up with unanswered calls, and if she knew this town the way she thought she did, news of her accident would have already hit the Grace phone wires.

She didn't realize she had clenched her eyes tight until she heard the truck tires crunch over the gravel driveway and felt the shuddering vibration of Quentin killing the engine.

"You can do this, Savannah."

His deep voice delivered the jolt she needed.

What did he know about what she could or couldn't do?

"Thanks for the ride." She hopped out of the truck, nearly twisting her ankle in the process, and stepped aside so Rocco could follow. As an ashamed afterthought, she mumbled, "Sorry about the crash."

"I'll go take care of your car. Okay if I swing back here after?" He grabbed her bag and delivered it to her. What was it about his movements that were so damned hypnotizing?

"No, don't. Go back to doing whatever it is you do." Quentin raised his eyebrow and gave a smile that didn't reach his eyes.

"I don't know why you're being so hostile to me. I didn't make you crash."

She fiddled with the strap of her duffel bag. He was right—she had no right to be hostile. He had been nothing but kind to her since their rude reunification. He couldn't be expected to know that she blamed him for his part in the death of her brother. Surely he had moved on with his life. Whose fault was it that she couldn't?

"You're right. I'm sorry." She stared at his truck, noticing the booster seat in the back and the sticky smudges on the rear windows. Before she could give in to the temptation to ask him about it, she clamped her jaw shut.

The less she knew about Quentin's life, the better. None of it was any of her business.

A door creaking open distracted her from her thoughts. Quentin's head nodded toward the door in greeting. She slowly turned, reminding herself that she could, in fact, do this.

Seeing her stepfather standing on the front steps nearly brought tears to her eyes. Not that she ever cried—she wasn't capable of such. Crying brought relief, or so she was told, and she had long ago vowed that she'd punish herself until the day she died.

"See you later, Peaches."

She wanted to jump back into his truck, beg him to drive until the memory of this town, her family, her baby brother were all behind her. But she knew from experience there was no place that far. She also knew no one could save her from herself.

Rick, her stepfather, opened his arms and stepped toward her. Her skin rebelled at the thought of undeserved affection from these familiar strangers— the people who should hate her even more than she hated herself. To sidestep it, she gathered her bag to her chest as if it were a heavy load and whistled to Rocco.

"Is he friendly?" Rick had the same nervous expression everybody had when confronted with Rocco for the first time.

"Yeah, he's great. Don't worry about him."

"I wasn't worried." His smile lit up his face, warming Savannah's heart the slightest bit. "Come on in. Your mother can't wait to see you."

"I bet," Savannah mumbled, trying her best not to let her negativity infect Rick. He was too good of a man to be brought to her low level.

The house smelled the same—a mixture of lemon

and vinegar and something sweet. The scent nearly knocked her over with painful memories of the time she had spent here. Careless days of running through the house, friends in tow. Shouting over her shoulder that she'd be back "sometime." Ignoring her mother's warnings that she'd better be home by curfew "or else." Without thinking, Savannah's eyes went to the spot over the mantle where pictures always hung. Sure enough, there was an extra large photo of Brandon's sweet face; his eight-year-old smile frozen in time. Her gut tightened at the unanticipated assault. All warmth drained from her extremities as her heart pounded in her chest.

"What is that creature doing here?" Karyn, Savannah's mother, startled Savannah with her directness. A moment passed before she realized her mother was referring to Rocco and not her.

Savannah wiped the gathering sweat from her forehead.

"Ri—Dad said I could bring him. Is that a problem?"

Her mother *hmmphed*. Some things never changed.

"I couldn't leave him alone. He's very friendly and well-behaved."

"You know I hate dogs." Karyn dissolved into a coughing fit, leaving Savannah unsure about… everything. Comfort her? Hug her? Rub her back? Get her water?

"I'll go stay someplace else." Savannah moved toward the door with Rocco following at her heels, his giant tongue flapping. Rick intervened as she reached for the door handle.

"Savvy, please don't hold her attitude against her. She's not been herself with all the meds."

"Seems like herself to me. Exactly as I remember her, actually."

"We want you to stay. She'll get used to your dog. Maybe we can keep him in the kitchen until she warms to the idea."

"I appreciate the offer, but Rocco belongs with me." After all the time the poor boy spent roaming the town in search of someone to love him, Savannah was incapable of treating him like anything less than a cherished member of her family. They were twin souls—stray, unloved, accepted only by each other.

Karyn's now-hoarse voice screeched from the living room. "That animal is not going in any carpeted areas!"

Rick bowed his head as though ashamed. Sweat glistened on his brow. The woman was probably driving the poor man insane.

"Here. Stay at the studio, then. And take my car. I heard what happened to yours." Rick unhooked a simple keychain from the hook next to the door.

"I couldn't."

"You must. I insist." He smiled, and she couldn't ignore the tears gathering in his eyes. He grabbed her hand in his, catching her off-guard. His hands were warm and rough and fatherly, just like always. "Please."

Hadn't she hurt him enough? The man who had

always loved her and treated her like his own flesh and blood; the man who had given her more warmth than her mother ever had. She was responsible for the death of his son—his only biological child. The least she could do was resist the urge to run away and potentially kill his wife in the process.

Hesitantly, she grabbed the keys he offered, clasping them in her fist. He smiled and sniffled.

"Thank you. I don't know what I'd do without the hope you're offering." Rick rubbed his eyes with his dry-skinned knuckles. "Your mother is grateful, too. Don't let her crankiness fool you."

Her mother had nothing to be grateful toward Savannah for. They didn't even know if Savannah's bone marrow would be a match. With her luck, her mother would be worse off if she received the transfusion.

She ducked her head. "Thanks for the keys."

"If you need anything, just holler."

Heart pounding, Savannah led Rocco to her stepfather's gray sedan. Rocco happily jumped into the front seat, eager for another driving adventure, while Savannah tossed her bag in the back. So far her precious pup seemed immune to the negativity of the day.

Not having a clue where she should go or what she should do, she found herself driving aimlessly through town. She fiddled with the radio when she was at a stop sign—she had no interest in the world news channel her stepdad had been listening to. She had enough trouble in her world without absorbing all the global negativity.

The urge to drive to the highway was strong. Her feet itched for a run. Her mind begged for caffeine.

"What do you think, my warrior? Are you in the mood for an afternoon snack?" Rocco wagged his tail stump at the promise of food. "A nice walk, a little nutritional boost, and then we'll find a hotel for the night."

Two hours later, Savannah was hit with the painful reality that no hotel in the world (or at least in the greater Healing Springs area) would accept a Rottweiler as a boarder. Not even with the promise of an extra large security deposit. Her savings account didn't have a very large cushion, anyway.

She parked the borrowed car in front of the coffee shop and watched the sun set over the building. She pushed her seat back, propped her knees up against the steering wheel, and scratched Rocco's ear.

What to do, what to do?

A vehicle pulled up beside her, and she tried to ignore it. Rocco refused to allow her, though, clambering over her to get to her open window.

"What are you so interested in out there?"

She hid her face in Rocco's fur when she glanced out the window and saw who was walking toward her car.

"Following me around, I see." Quentin's velvet tones washed over her, making her sink further into her seat.

"I was here first. But yeah, twice in one day. How lucky for me." She couldn't keep the sarcasm from her

Not Over You

voice. "How'd you know it was me?"

Quentin laughed. "I make it my business to know what all the beautiful women are up to in town."

She snorted. "I bet."

Quentin reached through the window to give Rocco the scratching he begged for. His clean, woodsy scent—a scent she could never erase from her olfactory memory—filled her with a longing she wanted to deny. Being close to her high school sweetheart, the one love of her life, was dangerous. Especially since he had clearly moved on and made a new world for himself, if the booster seat in the truck was any indication. She highly doubted he was a babysitter.

"What are you doing out here at dinnertime, anyway? I figured Rick would be spoiling you rotten with his homemade mac and cheese."

"That arrangement didn't work out." Savannah rolled her eyes at herself. Why was she unloading her private business to him?

Rocco chose that moment to move to the back seat, his attention drawn to something she couldn't understand. Savannah was now open and bared to Quentin. No more hiding behind the dog.

He leaned against the open window, his arms crossed and resting *right there.* She needed space. She needed oxygen. She needed to get away from his intoxicating presence.

"You can stay with me."

She laughed.

"I'm sure your wife would love that."

"There's no wife."

A bubble of something—excitement? Happiness?—grew inside her gut, completely unbidden.

"Girlfriend, then."

"Nope. Not even that." He smiled, and gosh darn it, she wanted to jump through the window and claim those lips as hers before someone else could.

"Well thanks anyway, but Rick gave me the key to the studio."

"That old place? It's practically falling apart. And it's in the middle of nowhere."

"Has the crime rate risen in Healing Springs over the last decade?" She raised her eyebrows and grinned. "From what I remember, the worst thing that ever happened was stolen lawn ornaments from time to time. And those usually showed up on someone else's lawn as a prank."

His eyes narrowed. "There's always a first time for everything. Never know."

"I appreciate your concern, but I have my own personal security system, anyway." She couldn't remember the last time she had felt her eyes crinkle in a smile. His unexpected protectiveness was kind of adorable.

"Well I'm coming with you to check things out. No one has been there since your mom got sick. I'll make sure no opportunists moved in."

"Really?" She sat up and leaned her elbow on the steering wheel. Was he serious?

"There could be mice." His arguments were

Not Over You

getting weaker, but his expression was getting cuter. "I think I can handle it. It takes more than a mouse to scare me off."

"Okay, but if you get there and discover that skunks have decided to nest in the couch, feel free to call me." He reached in to grab her cell from the dashboard. Without asking, he programmed his number in.

After a quick goodbye, she pulled out of the spot and drove to the outskirts of town to the dirt road that led to the studio.

She wasn't a bit surprised to see truck headlights pull into the driveway behind her.

Chapter Two

"All is clear," Quentin shouted from the creaky porch. He had insisted on going in ahead of Savannah, and since Rocco was doing the pee-pee shuffle, she let Quentin show off his manliness while she allowed Rocco to do his thing.

"Are you sure? Did you check the closets?"

"Of course."

"Did you check the shower?"

"Naturally."

"Did you check under the bed?"

Silence.

"I'll be right back."

Laughing to herself, she entered the studio for the first time. The musty inside was a stark contrast to the woodsy loveliness of outdoors. Mixed in with the thick scent of dust and mildew was the unforgettable smell of her mother's paint. Quentin had turned on all of the lights in the cabin, illuminating the easels and canvases around the room. Savannah didn't want to look, didn't want to see the depths of her mother's artistic soul, yet she was drawn to a particular canvas near the window.

Blue paint splattered in the middle looked like what may have been intended to represent a lake. That's how Savannah interpreted it, anyway. Screaming faces, elongated and translucent, hovered around the blue. Tree branches extended toward the lake, pulling, rescuing, failing.

"Hey, I found where she keeps the sheets."

Quentin's voice pulled her away from the horrific painting. She couldn't deny she was grateful for his presence—the perfect distraction.

"Oh, good. That mattress looks like it's seen better days."

He opened the sheet, parachuting it over the mattress. She grabbed a corner and together they struggled to finagle the musty smelling fabric into place.

"You sure you don't want to stay with me?"

When he looked at her like that, with his brown wavy hair falling over his forehead, she wanted nothing more than to stay with him. In his bed. On his kitchen table. In his truck. However he wanted her.

But she wasn't here to drudge up memories.

"A little perfume and some airing out will do the trick. But thanks."

"This bed holds special memories." His voice was deeper, huskier. Was he flirting with her?

She didn't respond. She knew exactly what memories he was speaking of.

He continued, seemingly oblivious to her silence.

"If I remember correctly, and I'm positive I do, you

gave me the greatest gift here on this bed."

"Oh hush, not in front of my dog." She whipped a blanket at him, which he diverted away from his face.

"The beautiful gift of your pure flower."

"My flower?" Savannah laughed. Was he kidding?

"You wanted me to talk in code."

"I didn't want you to talk at all." She hadn't smiled this much in ages. He had such a strange effect on her.

"Well, that day was the best. I wasn't even expecting it."

"I could tell…"

"Hey, you can't expect to catch a guy off-guard like that and have a miraculous experience."

She raised an eyebrow at him and let out a soft giggle.

"Besides, it was my first time, too." Defensiveness crept into his tone, but his body huffed up like he was ready to play offense.

He moved around to her side of the bed, looking like a cat on the prowl. She searched for Rocco, her protector, who at the moment was too busy licking his privates to give a flying fig about her personal safety.

Quentin was in touching distance. Distraction, distraction. She grabbed a pillow and attempted to shove the pathetic cushion into a threadbare pillowcase. *Why won't it go in?*

His breath warmed her ear as he leaned in, his words a caress. "I do recall you enjoying yourself quite a bit, though. I also remember something about whipped cream."

She cleared her throat. She was the one who

seduced when she had a need to fill or a memory to drown. She didn't like the powerlessness she felt at his intensity.

But try telling that to her body, which was responding like Publisher's Clearing House was at the door telling her she won the lottery.

The sexy man lottery.

The pillow and case slipped from her hand, tumbling to the bed. Her body turned toward him. She was powerless to stop it. Her heart raced, blood rushed south, her cheeks filled with heat. She couldn't remove her gaze from his lips. His luscious, soul-crushing, heart-blazing, delicious...

Rocco chose that moment to become the protector she no longer wanted him to be. Finally sensing Savannah's unease, he leapt to her side, growling a warning to Quentin. At the same time, Quentin's cell phone vibrated.

He cleared his throat and licked his lips.

"Peaches, I'm so sorry. I have to take this. I'm on call."

"Yeah, of course." She shook her head to clear the lust-daze, turning back to the pillow. She'd never get any sleep tonight.

"I have to run. There's an emergency."

"Go, go."

He kissed her on the forehead, pierced her with his longing gaze, scratched Rocco right where he liked to be scratched (making Savannah painfully envious in the process), and then left.

She tossed herself on the bed, covered her face

with the pillow, and cursed herself for being a fool.

***

If the sunlight streaming across her face wasn't bad enough, Rocco's thick tongue lapping her eyelids made Savannah want to bury her head under the smelly sheets and never rise.

Why did the bed have to be next to the one window where sunlight could peer through the trees? Savannah vowed to move the rickety bed if she had to spend one more night here.

Rocco groaned and pawed at her arm. "Okay, okay. I'll take you out."

Her needy pet jumped to the floor and pattered to the door. She stumbled across the way, shoving her feet into her tennis shoes but not bothering to straighten the heel.

Normally she was up at the crack of dawn, ready to go for an early morning run before the families took over the beach in the ocean town she lived in. But being here with all the memories trying to fight their way into her mind and her heart... she figured sleep was a good way to fend off the emotions.

"Let's make this quick." Rocco ran to the nearest tree. Savannah paced the small porch, noticing the aging and imperfections she had missed last night. The same little two-seater swing hung from the porch ceiling. Pots full of dirt and weeds lined the perimeter—clearly neglected. On the other side of the front door were two stacked plastic tubs. They didn't fit in with the rest of the cabin... they looked new. Clean. Bright. Everything this cabin was not.

She moved closer to study the mysterious tubs. No dust, no dirt, just one random pine needle that had probably blown off the rail.

She opened the tub. She recognized the handwriting on the note before she even lifted it. Ten years later and some things stayed the same.

"Since you didn't want to stay with me, I thought you might at least be able to use some fresh linens. But if you change your mind, the offer is always open. Forever, Q."

Savannah hugged the note to her chest. Why was he being so nice?

Rocco came bounding up the stairs, running to her legs, back down the stairs, around the trees, back to her. Over and over. She smiled at his energetic burst.

"I know. You want your morning run. Let me see what we can muster up for breakfast first." She had enough of his food in her duffel bag for a couple of days, but she'd need to make more soon. As for her, she might have a granola bar in the bottom of her purse. She had planned to stay with her parents and hadn't thought far enough ahead last night to realize she should pick up some groceries.

She dug through the tubs, smiling at Quentin's generosity and thoughtfulness. He had packed luxurious sheets, pillow cases, two fluffy towels, a stack of washcloths, a coloring book with a baggie of crayons (with a note attached saying, "in case you get bored"), and she thought she'd run to wherever he lived to kiss him when she got to the bottom tub. Her stomach growled when she started digging through the stack of breakfast bars, apples, instant oatmeal, and bottles of water.

On the very bottom was another note, written in red crayon. "I hope these things can sustain you for a little while. If you'd like a home-cooked meal, give me a call."

Was he offering to cook for her? The only time she could remember him cooking was one time when he had tried to make her a romantic dinner and he burned the pasta so badly the fire department had responded.

She grabbed a granola bar and bit into it as she went back inside to change. Rocco ran in beside her, looking at her like she was betraying him for eating without him. She dutifully filled his travel bowl before going about the rest of her morning routine. Fifteen minutes later, they were ready for their exercise.

At home, she preferred to run on the beach. The ocean waves always soothed her soul and invigorated her. Here, however, the lake held too many memories—toxic, painful memories. Memories of her brother's death.

Her feet hit the wooded path in the opposite direction, carrying her away from the pain. Her ear buds blocked out the sound of her own screams from ten years ago. She dodged low-lying branches, leapt over rocks and roots, and did her best to become one with the forest.

If she had to be back in this town, she might as well make the best of it. She'd run by that old house she had grown up fantasizing about—the giant Victorian with the purple shutters. It was always so out of place on the wooded lot. The yard had been filled with gorgeous gardens, and the lake was only a short walk from the back yard. Back then there had been a private beach area for that house.

Rocco alerted her that someone was nearby by nudging against her leg and then moving behind her. She slowed her pace, not wanting to knock anyone over by accident. She yanked her buds out of her ears when Rocco went running ahead. She called to him, but he didn't stop; he refused to listen.

She ran to catch up, surprised to see Quentin bending down to greet Rocco. That little traitor... he ignored her for *him?*

"What are you doing out here?" She panted, bending over with her hands on her knees, desperately trying to ward off a cramp. She forgot to grab water in her haste to get running.

"I was on my way to check on you, actually." He stood to his full height of six foot two. She straightened, too, brushing the hairs that had escaped her ponytail out of her sweaty face.

"This is kind of a strange way to get to the studio. Why didn't you drive over? Or call?"

"It's easier to walk—I live right there." He nodded toward the very house of her dreams.

"No way. Did they turn it into apartments?"

"No. I bought it."

He bought it? He bought that gorgeous mini-mansion? The one she had cuddled up to him and told him they would live in one day? The one he had promised he'd buy for her?

A lump clogged her throat. She didn't quite know how to react. Did he remember those summer nights sneaking onto the private dock? Did he remember how she'd write naughty short stories about the gardens and leave them in his locker?

Or did he just like the house?

His intense stare penetrated her all the way to the deep ball of regret and remorse lodged in her gut. Scar tissue had grown over the parts of her heart capable of loving and being loved, but that didn't stop the erratic organ from pumping more than it should.

She caught her body leaning forward and quickly corrected her posture.

Quentin cleared his throat and shoved his hands in his pockets.

"Anyway, I wanted to see if you needed anything. Groceries, a place to stay," he smiled around his words, "a kitchen to use. Does that old microwave even work anymore?"

"I haven't tried it yet. Thank you for the special delivery, by the way."

Quentin picked up a stick and threw it for Rocco, who caught it and then settled down to chew it to bits.

"He's not much for fetch, huh?"

She laughed at the suggestion. "Um, no. Definitely not." She watched Rocco chomp and chew for a few moments, not sure what to say. "No work today?" Lame, but what do you say to the man who commanded such mixed emotions and past regrets?

"I'm pretty much always on call since I'm the only paramedic. We don't have much go on around here most days, but I do respond to other towns when there's a big trauma."

"I thought you wanted to be a big business guy."

"Things change." Something passed over his expression—a deep pain she recognized. "Besides, who says I'm not? Maybe I have many layers." He winked.

The image of his layers peeling off nearly sent her reeling. Hot damn. Maybe this time the fire department would be responding to her internal flames.

She didn't want the fire fighters, though. No, her body only had this magnetic connection to one paramedic. And she was sure there was nothing in his first aid kit that could make her better, so she knew she had to keep a safe distance. And maybe wear a helmet. Or a chastity belt. Or handcuffs and a whip.

Dammit!

Her phone buzzed from the armband she used for running. Grateful for the distraction, she excused herself and listened to the voicemail from her stepfather. He was asking for her to pick up some books or magazines for her mother and to come over for lunch.

"I have to go. Rick needs me to run some errands."

Since she was in town to help out, she couldn't politely refuse.

"Of course. If you need to get into the house and I'm not there, just go ahead in. It's open."

"Thanks." She tapped her leg to call Rocco to attention, offered the best smile she was capable of, and ran back toward the studio.

She never did get to see the house.

***

Quentin watched her run away, her ponytail dancing from side to side, her muscular thighs contracting as she moved. Gone was the vibrant young girl he remembered. She was a shell of her former self. Polite, but distant. She looked the same—better, actually—but she harbored a deep sadness he could feel every time he was with her.

In spite of her sadness, their sexual attraction hadn't dimmed the slightest bit.

When Rick first told Quentin about Savannah's imminent return, Quentin hadn't known what to think or feel about it. Elation? Yes. Terror? Absolutely.

Savannah had run away ten years ago, right before her high school graduation. She hadn't been able to deal with the sudden death of her eight-year-old brother, and if Quentin's feelings toward the event were any indication, she more than likely blamed herself. He had gone through years of counseling to correct this misperception, but he guessed she hadn't.

Quentin searched for her for years. He hated the thought that something terrible had happened to her. He didn't want to live without her. Not only were they high school sweethearts—they had been soul mates. Best friends. She accepted him regardless of his shitty family situation. She loved him for who he was, not what everyone thought he should be. He wanted to heal together, just like they did everything else.

But she had run. She hadn't even told him she was going.

Six years ago, when he had made some good money in his investments and could finally afford to hire someone to find her, he did indeed locate her.

He even drove there, to a tourist trap in Maine.

He saw her.

And then he left.

She had moved on with her life. She hadn't appeared happy, but she was settled. She was cared for. She was on her own.

He had wanted to beg her to come back. To scream at her for leaving. To cry about how much he had missed her.

Instead, his youthful pride had won and he came home and fell into a trap of his own.

Now she was here, and he hoped their little town of Healing Springs would work its magic on her heart.

Lost in thought and memories, he didn't hear the crunch of leaves until she was a few paces away.

"Couldn't resist seeing me again?" He joked, clearing the cobwebs of regret out of his mind.

"Actually, I do have a super huge favor."

"Anything." He meant it.

She looked around curiously.

"Why are you still standing in the same place?"

Because I was lost in thoughts of you.

"I like the peace and quiet of the woods."

"Oh, yeah. Me, too." She didn't look convinced, if her wrinkled brow and suspicious eyes were any indication. "Anyway, I only packed enough food for Rocco for a couple of days, figuring I could make more at my parent's house. Since I'm not staying there and I don't think she'd be thrilled about me using her kitchen..." Her voice trailed off and she drew her bottom lip between her teeth.

"Wait, you make your dog's food?" He stifled a grin. She had been about as far from domesticated as you could get. The thought of her making anyone food reminded him how many years had passed.

"Yes, I do." She straightened her shoulders and raised her chin. "It's healthier that way."

"Dogs will eat garbage if you let them."

"I would never let him. He deserves the best."

"I suppose you feed him all organic ingredients, too?" He thought he was joking, but judging by the redness in her cheeks and her unwillingness to look him in the eye, he'd say his joke hit the mark of reality. "You're kidding."

"Don't you watch the news? Have you not heard of all the poisonings from animal food companies? No way."

She brought her hands to her hips and stared at him until he stopped laughing. When he could regain his composure, he said, "You are more than welcome to use my kitchen. Anytime."

"Thank you." She turned to run off once again. Before she took off, she asked, "Maybe tomorrow?"

"Tomorrow would be perfect."

Not Over You

He couldn't understand the physical reaction he was having to the thought of her coming to his house. For Christ's sake, she was going to be making dog food in his kitchen, not playing wifey.

But his heart—not to mention his painful erection—couldn't tell the difference.

Chapter Three

After a freezing cold shower (she'd have to figure out what the deal was with the hot water heater, but in the meantime, she kind of needed a cold shower after running into Quentin again, anyway), she harnessed Rocco and drove into town. No use delaying what needed to be done.

Rocco tried to chew at the harness the entire drive. "I know you don't like it, but people are afraid of big dogs. Not everyone knows you here, you know. Besides, you won't be allowed in the stores, so I need to tie you up outside. It will only be for a few minutes, I promise."

Rocco gave her his sad little puppy dog eyes, and she felt like a terrible caregiver for even suggesting leaving him outside. But the late May heat was too strong to leave him in the car, and health laws were health laws. (Though she personally could think of many people who were more unsanitary than her well-cared-for dog. If only she could rule the world…)

Finding a spot was surprisingly easy, but she supposed tourist season wasn't in full swing yet. Since

Healing Springs was named for a supposedly mystical spring that could cure all ailments, the town saw its share of visitors throughout the year. Add in the fact that the small town was centrally located to the mountains, many lakes, a world-class bike path, and much more, summer months could become unbearable.

She grabbed her baseball cap and tucked her ponytail through the back opening. If she kept the visor down, maybe no one would recognize her. She'd be in and out and back to the car in no time.

"Well knock me off my rocker," Mrs. Reynolds called out the second Savannah walked through the annoying door filled with bells of all sizes. "Just look at you. Savannah Grace. I thought I'd be six feet under before you'd finally come home."

Savannah forced a smile as the elderly woman pushed her walker to meet Savannah where she stood. How lucky for her that she made it in the store for precisely five seconds before her anonymity was shattered.

"Hi, Mrs. Reynolds." Savannah smiled, hoping her discomfort didn't show. The old woman had always been painfully astute. Savannah didn't want her emotions read by anyone—particularly someone who knew her tragic story. "How did you know it was me?"

"Oh, child, I'd never forget your look. We've missed you around here. Have you seen Quentin yet?" The woman's wrinkled eyes twinkled. Forever the town's matchmaker, she had the uncanny ability to see directly into people's hearts and souls. She had successfully matched dozens of couples—or so legend had it.

She was way off base if she was trying to match Savannah up with anyone, especially Quentin.

"That boy has developed into quite the fine young man. Nice ass on him, too."

Savannah blinked at the elderly woman. Surely she had heard her wrong.

"Mrs. Reynolds! You've become even more lecherous in your golden years, haven't you?" Savannah smiled and winked back at the old woman.

"Oh, you know it." Mrs. Reynolds leaned forward as though about to divulge a great secret. "That's what keeps women young, you know. Can't kill the libido!"

Savannah laughed. "I'll take your word on that."

Mrs. Reynolds looked past Savannah.

"Is that your dog out there? What a beast!"

"He's a good dog," Savannah blurted. People were so quick in their judgments about him.

"Never said he wasn't. My husband raised Rotties in his day. Good dogs. Protective, too." She turned to Savannah and peered directly into her eyes. "Not a good replacement for a man, though."

Savannah nearly choked. She coughed into her elbow, wishing she could undo this entire conversation. She should have planned better. She could have brought a wig. She could have had plastic surgery to alter her face. She could have hired someone to run her errands while she awaited the blood work.

She should have thought this through.

"I suppose you didn't come in here just to see little old me. What can I help you find?"

"It's wonderful to see you, Mrs. Reynolds," Savannah lied. Well, it wasn't exactly a *lie*—not in the hurtful sort of way. Savannah had nothing against the old lady. She was rather fond of her, actually. She just couldn't stand jumping through the looking glass and winding up in Miseryland. "I need some light reading for my mother."

Mrs. Reynolds went right to work directing Savannah to the books she personally recommended for Karyn Grace. She knew that Karyn had been reading a particular series, so she encouraged Savannah to pick up the next book.

Savannah grabbed a few magazines that looked mom-friendly, paid, and then said her goodbyes as she returned to her panting dog.

"Our fun has just begun, my warrior prince." Rocco danced his front paws around as Savannah unhooked him from the old-fashioned hitching post on the sidewalk in front of the shop. She wished she had a dog's proclivity for not knowing how much life sucked.

"Oh yes, you think you're going to have a grand old time. Little do you know how horrible things shall get in the Grace household."

She wished she hadn't promised to visit for lunch. She had felt pressured by her stepfather. She knew her mother would rather gouge out her own eyes than have her murderous daughter sharing a table with her, but she couldn't exactly bring that up, especially in front of Quentin.

Savannah eyed the Healing Springs tavern, carefully and privately tucked away down a little lane between some of the bigger stores. She wished she could grab a drink in the tiny bar before facing her family again, but only the most hard-core townie drunks would be in there this time of day.

Instead, she walked the proverbial plank and drove her stepdad's car back to his house, carefully avoiding any landmarks that would trigger painful memories.

***

"So glad you made it," Rick said as he swept Savannah into his embrace. She tried to hug back, but he had hugged her over her arms.

When he pulled away, she held out the bag of books. "Here ya go."

"Go ahead and bring them to your mother. I have to flip the steaks. Does Rocco want to come and grill with me? There might be a dropping or two..."

"I'm sure he'd love that." Savannah dreaded facing her mother without any security blanket, but what could she say?

Rick pushed the door open, gesturing for Savannah to enter.

She tiptoed into the house. When she couldn't find her mother immediately, she began to search. There she was, in the library/den, sitting in a rocking chair, looking out the window to the yard. Savannah stood behind her, marveling at the changes. Gone was the wooden swing set—the one with the plastic climbing wall and monkey bars Brandon had been so excited to get for his seventh birthday. The giant sandbox with the construction trucks was gone, too. Even the tire swing that once hung from the ancient oak had been erased from view. In their place were sophisticated gardens and statues. No children would play here.

While her mother sat silent, Savannah had the niggling feeling that she had intruded on a private bubble of reflection. She quietly moved backward, intending to reenter the room with an announcement that she was here.

"Leaving so soon?" Savannah froze in place. "Always running away, aren't you?"

So her mother had known she was there. Shame flushed Savannah's face and chest.

"I wasn't leaving. I felt like I was intruding on a private moment."

Her mother rose from her chair—a bit wobbly, but with stiff shoulders.

"Come. We'll make some tea."

Karyn's regal posture was the same, though her pace was slower. Her hair no longer flowed down her back, but even in its short style, it was well-coifed and under control. Savannah couldn't recall a time when Karyn had seemed human. Flaws were not something she believed in, nor something she seemed to possess. Definitely not something she allowed or accepted in her daughter.

"I brought you some things to read." Savannah spoke over the lump in her throat.

"You can leave them there by my chair."

Savannah complied before following her mother into the kitchen. Savannah watched her mother move with grace around the small room—reaching up to retrieve dainty tea cups, preparing the tea bags, pouring sugar into the porcelain serving container. Karyn refused Savannah's help, so Savannah stood to the side, trying to stay out of the way.

Like she did throughout her teen years.

"Where's that creature of yours?"

"Rocco is out with Dad."

"Rocco? What kind of name is that?" Karyn pulled milk from the refrigerator.

"The kind my dog has."

At Savannah's snarky tone, Karyn glared at her.

"Don't be getting smart with me in my own house."

Savannah clenched her jaw so tight, she heard it pop.

"If you don't want me here, just say so. It was Dad's suggestion for me to come over, not mine."

Karyn turned away from Savannah to the teacups on the counter. Savannah noticed her mother's shoulders lean forward the slightest bit. Her hands shook as she poured water into one cup. Before Savannah could develop any crazy ideas about her mother's vulnerability, Karyn turned to her with a completely neutral expression.

"If you don't care to be here, just go."

Rick came in as Savannah and her mother stared each other down. Rocco padded over the mustard-colored tiles, oblivious to the tension between mother and daughter.

"Woo! Should I go to the shed to get the chainsaw to cut the tension in here? What is going on with you girls?" Rick held out a tray of teriyaki-marinated steak—Savannah recognized the smell. Her favorite from summertime barbecues. She hadn't had it since she moved away.

"That smells delicious," Savannah said, breaking the silence.

"Well come on over and have a seat. Rocco approved."

"You gave that animal our meal?" Karyn sneered.

"Oh, relax, my darling. It was a tiny bit." Rick winked at Savannah, leaving her to suspect that the portion was anything but tiny. She'd have to be sure to take him for another run later.

"Now if you two wouldn't mind, I'm starving."

Savannah called a mental cease-fire with her mother and followed her stepdad into the dining room. Rocco padded along, sitting behind her chair.

Karyn glared at the dog, making him growl. She growled back. But she didn't demand that he leave.

Karyn remained silent throughout the meal. Rick and Savannah made small talk, both of them careful to avoid any discussion of the past.

Karyn ended her silence as Savannah prepared to leave.

"Have you been to his stone?"

The words, calculated and calm, froze Savannah in her tracks.

The delightful meal Rick had provided threatened to make a reappearance. Her eyes darted around the room, searching for an easy escape. She wished for a distraction, something to take the heat off her. Something to hide her sins.

Rick sensed her angst and moved over to put his hand over her shoulders. "It was great to see you, sweetie. I forgot to mention, I spoke to Hal about your car. He said he's happy to fix it up without going through your insurance. He owes me a favor."

Savannah swallowed past the pain and discomfort. She took a deep breath, promised herself she'd go for a run, and managed to mumble a quiet, "Thank you."

"Don't mention it, sweetie. Until the parts come in, you go ahead and use my car. Everything okay at the old studio?"

Savannah nodded. She couldn't shake her mother's hard stare. She didn't blame the woman for hating her, but Savannah didn't plan to put herself on the stake for her mother to light a match to Savannah's shame.

"I'll walk you to your car. Karyn, say your goodbyes now, my darling."

His darling did no such thing. She turned her back and meandered away, disappearing to another room. But not before she narrowed her eyes at Savannah one last time.

**

Not Over You

Since no radio stations in this blasted town had music angry enough to soothe her nerves, Savannah took her anger out on her eardrums. The loud music blared in her ears—better to protect Rocco from the noise, anyway. She sang at the top of her lungs, banging on the steering wheel for emphasis. She didn't care when people looked at her funny as she drove down the road. She laughed at the worried look she received from someone at the four way stop sign (and if she wasn't mistaken, the other driver had been her high school biology teacher. Good, let him worry about how she turned out.)

Everyone had their opinions about her, anyway. She was sure of it.

Rocco reached his head over to her lap. She rubbed his ears, thankful for his presence. After three raging metal songs, she slipped the buds out of her ears and gave her attention to her dog and the road.

Where had she driven herself to while lost in rage?

Shivers wracked her body. Her eyes turned into crazed search and rescue beacons. She shifted into reverse, preparing to do a three-point turn to get off this dead end.

And wouldn't it be her luck that Rocco started begging to go out at that very moment?

"You can wait."

He disagreed. He barked at her, sending goosebumps over her arms. She didn't want to get out of the car here.

Rocco started clawing at the door. He wasn't used

to eating steak or the marinade Rick had used, so there was a good chance he truly was desperate to go.

Savannah swore under her breath and pulled to the side of the small dirt road.

"You are so lucky I love you." She glared at her dog as she let him out. He immediately ran to the woods.

"No, Rocco!"

He disappeared into the wooded play area. She heard the birds squawking at his interruption, the crunch of the pine needles as he ran. Her feet, however, had grown roots.

What if kids were playing over there? It was a weekday during school hours, but that didn't mean parents couldn't be there with younger children. All she needed was for one of the yuppy parents to be scared of Rocco and report them to animal control. She wanted to make as few waves as possible while she was here.

She squared her shoulders and marched down the small path. She'd have a little talk with her pet about his rebellion later.

She spotted Rocco right away, but her attention immediately went to the unchanged play area.

This type of area was unique to her small town. When she was a teenager, she had volunteered to help build it. Someone had envisioned a natural playground without all the plastic and pressurized wood that made up other playgrounds. This one was a peaceful oasis where kids could be kids. Where their imaginations could soar. Where they could be the kings and queens of the universe.

Not Over You

Brandon's favorite place in the whole world, aside from the lake.

She rubbed her arms. When had it become so chilly?

Savannah shuffled across the soft bed of pine needles that carpeted the forest floor. No one was here, but she could hear voices. Brandon's voice. Her teenage voice.

"Please can we play in the mud pit? Please? I won't get dirty!"

"Are you nuts? Mom will freak if I let you get your school clothes muddy again. Do you want me to be grounded for life?"

"She won't be mad."

"Yes she will. She won't be mad at you—she'll be mad at me, the one she hates."

Brandon bent his head to his chest.

"I guess you're right. I don't wanna get you in trouble."

Savvy studied his forlorn expression until her heart broke along with his.

"Okay, fine. You can play for five minutes. But please try not to fall in the mud again. Use a stick, take off your shoes, whatever. But stay as clean as possible."

Brandon wrapped his arms around her middle, squeezing tight. She pried him off and laughed as she sent him on his way.

Savannah found herself smiling at the memory. He

had, indeed, fallen in the mud. And she had, indeed, been called irresponsible and told she was grounded until she was eighteen. Luckily for her, her stepdad had intervened and soothed her mother's ruffled feathers. Savannah had gone out with her friends that weekend, just like always.

Savannah wandered over to the mud pit—that fun square filled with the softest dirt, which was fed with a pipe of water that created glorious mud during the entire warm season. One section was shallow enough to walk in with bare feet, letting the mud squish between toes for those inclined. The bravest could walk up to their knees in the mud. The most insane could take a full mud bath. Brandon especially loved the mud bath.

She looked to the side, where she noticed something that had never been there before.

In keeping with the theme of the area, it was an old, sliced tree stump with a carving that made her throat tighten and her heart swell.

Brandon Richard Grace
Forever Eight Years Old
May Your Heaven Be Filled With Mud and Trucks and Legos

Beneath the words, carved into the tree slice, was a familiar portrait of Brandon's angelic—and sometimes mischievous—face.

Savannah wondered who created such a wonderful memorial. Her mother would have never put such a sentiment on a tree stump. She didn't approve of him frolicking in nature. Her idea of memorializing the young boy would have been a fancy stone or a memorial wall at the school.

Savannah knelt before the stump, stunned. Rocco ran to her side and began licking her dry cheeks.

When Rocco first forced his way into her life, she would push him away when he comforted her. Over time, she gave in to his relentless need to drag her out of her darkest fogs. She'd never believe she deserved him, but she had grown to appreciate the companionship and acceptance.

Savannah wrapped her arms around her dog and buried her face in his neck.

He stood, stoically allowing her this moment of grief.

She didn't want to see his stone. That signified such cold, harsh reality. Permanency. A grown up world where her brother didn't belong. Here, in this place where she had bonded so well with her baby brother, is where she would always feel him. Where he belonged.

Savannah lost track of the time she spent at the mud pit and the tree stump. She only knew that her grief showed its ugly head for too long, and she had no right to grieve this way.

She stood up, ignoring the cramping of her thighs and her muddy knees. She jogged back to the car with Rocco at her heels, itching for a run through the woods.

She changed into running clothes in record time once she reached the studio. Adrenaline surged through her veins. She was feeling reckless. Impulsive. Ready to run until all thoughts were banished from her head.

She let the door flutter to a close behind her, and then slammed right into the hardest chest she had felt in her life.

Savannah jerked her head back and brought her hands to her aching nose. She didn't feel any blood gushing, so she must not have broken it on Quentin's steel pecs.

Quentin, ever the gentleman, reached out to steady her.

"Are you okay?"

He studied her eyes as if checking for a concussion. His look of concern fed a hollow place deep in her gut. His hands on her arms and his body so close made her burn to be closer.

She knew she'd regret kissing him. But she also knew she'd regret the loss of this opportunity even more.

Chapter Four

One minute he's doing his best to come up with a good excuse for being on her front porch, the next minute Savannah is hurling herself into his arms, attacking his face with an all-consuming kiss.

Quentin reacted instantly. His hands on her lower back, he pulled her closer. She moaned deep into his mouth while her tongue danced a dance he had never forgotten.

He didn't mean to let passion take over, but he couldn't contain his urge to push her against the cabin, his body seeking, wanting, needing. His hands played in her silky hair. She tasted the same—ten years hadn't dimmed his body's memory of her. Her smell, her taste, the feel of her in his arms.

With her hands on his face, he was Superman. Leap tall buildings? Heck, yeah. Anything for her.

"Let's go in." Her words, a breathy whisper, penetrated the fog of his lust-drenched mind. "Let's do this."

She moved against him seductively, invitingly.

His body wanted to take her then and there.

He reached his hand up her shirt. Oh yes. Just as full as he remembered. Her nipples reacted to his attention instantly. His erection became more painful, straining against his zipper. She reached down, caressing him through his jeans, and he was afraid he'd embarrass himself if he didn't calm his raging thoughts.

He tried to slow the kisses, but she increased the tempo. He growled and gave in to the flow. His tongue made love to her mouth. She purred, arched her back, demanded more.

He moved his hand to the waistband of her running pants. His fingers teased the top of her panties. He could smell her desire, could feel her begging him to complete her.

He could also feel the intangible sadness he had felt in her since she arrived. Only this time, more powerful.

He stepped back, not letting go of her. He had to stop kissing her. She was intoxicating. Messing with his better judgment.

She looked up at him, confusion creating lines on her otherwise smooth forehead. Her eyes were still hooded with desire.

"Why'd you stop?" Her hands moved under his shirt, over his stomach, up his chest.

Ten years. He couldn't believe it had been ten damn years.

He grabbed her arms, stopping them from their pursuit. She scowled at him.

"I don't remember you having those washboard abs before," Savannah grinned. "Why are you hiding them from me?"

He couldn't help but smile back.

She took advantage of his weakness and pulled his head down to hers again.

He was lost in her kiss. No compass, no map, no clue when the storm would rush in and wash them away.

Savannah reached behind her and pushed the door to the studio open. He followed her in. He couldn't help it. He was firmly under her spell.

But when they weren't kissing, she was tense. Guarded. Emotionally unavailable.

He pulled away, harsher than he meant to be.

He turned toward the door, willing his erection to take a hike. Running his hand through his hair, he searched for something to say that wouldn't be misconstrued.

He wanted Savannah—damn, he had never wanted anyone more—but he had to respect her. She was clearly still mourning. Being here in town was distressing to her, and if he allowed himself to take advantage of her, he'd not only be a complete ass, but he'd deserve to lose her. Again.

"Peaches, I'm sorry. I shouldn't have done that."

No response.

He turned around, expecting to see tears in her eyes or an embarrassed face or a smile at the very least. In his experience, women didn't appreciate being rejected.

Nope. If reality was the moon, he was in another galaxy.

Her face was stone. Her eyes were hardened to him. The warm, affectionate woman who had thrown herself in his arms now stared at him like she would a stranger. She didn't glare. She didn't appear upset.

"I didn't come here to take advantage of you," he said, needing to reassure her. Or himself.

She reached up to her hair, adjusted her now-unkempt ponytail, said, "You didn't," then ran past him and into the woods.

Shit. What the hell had he done?

He watched as her dutiful dog, once distracted with a chew toy that had been on the floor of the porch, ran after her.

Quentin wanted to run, too. He wanted to chase her. To beg her to be his.

But she ran.

Away from him.

Like she did before.

He'd never stop loving her. Nor would he ever be unavailable to her.

But she would have to come to him.

***

Quentin gulped down the last of his third cup of coffee as he raced to answer the door. He would need a bucketful of caffeine to get through the day. Between his raging erection, lustful thoughts of Savannah all night long, and a bright and cheerful six-year-old waking him at the crack of dawn, he had maybe slept for a total of fifteen minutes.

Not Over You

He didn't realize he was still in his SpongeBob pajama pants and the Healing Springs Soccer League t-shirt he got roped into buying at the last fundraiser until he swung the door open.

"Hey, neighbor. Mind if I use your kitchen?" Savannah had two reusable shopping bags in her hands. She held them up and smiled. "I brought my own supplies."

"Yeah. Yeah, of course." Quentin stepped back to make room for her and her dog to enter. He had somehow managed to forget that she'd be coming today. He was stunned that she followed through. Especially after last night.

He watched the way she took quick possession of his kitchen. Did she own every space she entered?

She placed her bags on the counter and began unpacking them, lining up fresh veggies, packages of meat, and a giant bag of rice.

"Are you cooking for you? That's a great idea. You can reheat at the studio."

She looked over her shoulder and smiled.

"I'll have to come back another day for that. Today is all about Rocco."

He didn't know what to say. He suspected the dog ate better than he did.

"Are you sure this isn't an imposition?"

He shook his head. "Not at all. I want you here."

She lowered her eyes before he could read her reaction to his words. Not wanting to make a big deal of anything—clearly she planned to pretend nothing happened between them last night—he smiled and moved toward the counter, perusing the fresh foods.

"Organic? You weren't kidding, were you?"

She pursed her lips and tightened her jaw.

Sensing her anger rising, he knelt in front of Rocco. "You're the luckiest dog on the planet, aren't you?" Quentin rubbed Rocco's ears as the animal danced his back feet back and forth.

He felt Savannah relax. He enjoyed the way she began to hum as she worked. Unfortunately, he had to head out for a meeting before picking Joey up from his half-day at school.

"I have to jump in the shower—need anything?"

He watched her nibble on her lower lip and wondered if she had the same thoughts as he did.

He stepped closer. He couldn't help himself.

"Care to join me?"

She seemed tempted for a minute, but looked down at his SpongeBob pants.

He hadn't been this embarrassed since the time they went skinny dipping in high school and his so-called best friend stole his clothes from the shore. That was the first time Savannah had seen his pathetically skinny sixteen-year-old naked ass.

"Hey, I'll have you know—it takes a strong man to dress like a fool."

"I bet it does." She laughed through her words, widening her eyes in fake seriousness. "You must be a very strong man."

If it took dressing like a fool to bring out this joy in her, he'd do it every day. Her eyes sparkled, her teeth gleamed. Her delight tingled his skin.

Not Over You

"I don't want to brag, but I have been working out," Quentin said, flexing his muscles and walking toward her. "Wanna feel?"

He put his hands on her hips, turning her toward him. Her hands immediately went to his arms. She licked her lower lip before drawing it between her teeth. Her eyes stared at his chest. He swore he could feel her heart leaping from her shirt to his chest, but maybe that was his own?

He began to lower his head toward hers.

She cleared her throat and twisted away, mumbling something about having to stir the rice.

He stepped away, counting backwards by thirteen. *Calm yourself.* He wondered who was the real dog in this room.

"Quentin—"

"I'll be in the shower. Yell if you need anything." The cold shower. He wondered if she'd be suspicious if he grabbed a bucket of ice and brought it with him.

He was usually so in control of himself, of his feelings, of his libido. He had sworn off any serious relationships after what his ex-girlfriend pulled on him. After she abandoned their son and never even bothered to check in to see how he was, he realized he was cursed when it came to relationships. Casual hook-ups? Occasionally. But he had more important things to worry about, including his son.

Quentin could feel her eyes on him as he walked away. He didn't mean to be rude, but if he didn't get out of there soon, he might blast them to the past quicker than he should.

***

Savannah swore under her breath when she heard the water running. She shouldn't have come here. Sure, she had to make Rocco's food, but she knew as sure as she knew that her favorite color was green that she came here for one real reason.

She wanted to be near Quentin.

Okay, so he rejected her last night. So what? Maybe he was being shy. She knew he wanted her—she could feel the zap between them every time they were within ten feet of one another.

She covered the rice and checked the meat mixture. She probably could speed up the process, but she had a precise way of cooking that made her food unique and healthy. She hoped Quentin didn't mind her taking up the entire morning.

Savannah looked around at all the details in the kitchen. A handprint on blue construction paper that said "Happy Father's Day" in a young child's sloppy writing confirmed her suspicions. A train table tucked into a corner of the large kitchen made her smile. The home was neat and orderly, which surprised her. She knew Quentin loved kids and was good with them—he had spent a great deal of time with her while she was babysitting her little brother—but she had a hard time imagining him as a *dad.*

She heard Quentin opening a door down the hall, so she busied herself chopping vegetables.

Her body screamed with awareness when he

entered the kitchen. He smelled fresh and *delicious*. Oh, how she wished things were different and she could have joined him in the shower. She smiled at him when he grabbed a piece of carrot and popped it into his mouth. She wanted to catch the drop of water running from his hair to his forehead with her tongue. She wanted to taste him, own him.

Distracted, her knife slipped and she sliced her index finger. She swore before shoving it into her mouth to ease the pain.

Quentin sprang into action. He demanded that she show him her finger, then wrapped it and pulled a first aid kit out of the island drawer. She watched him as he worked. It was a tiny cut, barely any blood, but he worked with precision and authority. He wrapped the bandage around her finger and kissed it gently.

She melted.

Damn those brown eyes and the power they had on her. Why did his eyelashes have to be so damned seductive? Why did her body have to betray her so freaking much? Why couldn't she keep the distance her mind told her she should be keeping?

"I guess if I'm going to be careless, it's best to be around an EMT."

He smiled. Her knees weakened. She couldn't take her eyes off him.

"Paramedic, actually."

"Oh, excuse me." She rolled her eyes.

"You're forgiven. Just always remember one thing. I live to serve."

Yeah, he could serve her. On the counter. On the

floor. In his bedroom.

"I have to get going, though. I have a meeting."

His husky voice sent chills down her entire body, forcing her nipples into tight peaks that threatened to burst through her shirt and stab him until he helped her find completion.

"Oh, I'm sorry. I'll clean up."

"You finish what you're doing. I won't be gone long."

"Thank you."

He left her and Rocco alone in his kitchen.

She missed him as soon as he closed the door.

Chapter Five

Two hours later, Savannah was putting the finishing touches on the dog food when the front door swung open. She jumped, dropping one of her lids on the floor.

"I'll get it!" A cheerful voice shouted. She froze when she saw the brown-haired cherub rushing to her side, an eager look on his sweet face. She looked around the room, frantic, knowing she shouldn't be around children. She was a hazard.

Savannah double-checked the burner to be sure the boy couldn't get hurt. Did she leave the knife on the counter? Panic fueled her heart. Nope, it was already in the strainer, all washed. She willed herself to calm down before her anxiety created a storm.

The little boy reached up to place the lid on the counter.

"Thank you," Savannah squeaked out, her voice trembling a little.

Quentin strolled in, casually at first, but with a look of concern when he noticed her panic.

"Joey, go ahead and put your stuff away. I'll get your lunch ready."

Quentin's eyes didn't leave Savannah's. She didn't blame him for sending the kid away from her. She was a mess. And a killer.

Her hands shook as she began packing her things. She had cleaned up most of the kitchen, but still had to wipe down the counter.

Her adrenaline would probably help her whip through the rest of her tasks in three minutes or less. She could be out of there before the boy returned to the kitchen.

Quentin's hand stilled hers. She looked up at him, eyes wide and scared.

"I'll be out of here in a minute." She breathed deeply to avoid stuttering. "Sorry it took so long."

"You don't have to leave. Stay for lunch."

She shook her head, emotions she couldn't identify clogging her throat.

"Joey had a half day today, so he's eager for a special dad-made meal. His nanny usually cooks, but she's away this week."

Dad. Nanny. Domesticity.

She couldn't wrap her head around it all.

The boy returned faster than she anticipated.

Her stomach twisted in knots that would give a sailor a challenge. Vomit gathered in her throat. She had carefully avoided children. Even in the store she worked in—if a child entered the store, Valentina, the store owner, had learned to accept that Savannah would disappear into the back storage room.

Savannah pressed her hand to her chest. She needed to escape. Quentin leaned closer.

"He's just a child. He doesn't even bite anymore." He smiled, but this time it wasn't enough to settle her nerves.

The boy hopped like a frog over to Rocco, who immediately rolled onto his back to show submission. The boy screeched in excitement, rubbing the dog's belly with enthusiasm.

"Joey, you didn't ask if you could pet the dog."

"Can I play with the dog?" He didn't stop petting while he waited for the answer.

Savannah looked from the boy to Quentin, not knowing what to do, not able to speak. Quentin nodded, seemingly granting permission.

"He'd like that." She didn't know how the words managed to escape her clogged throat, but she was grateful they did. She couldn't be rude to a child. She didn't want to be, anyway.

Lost in her own misery, she watched as the boy brought a ball to toss for Rocco. While Rocco would happily chase it, he wouldn't bring it back to the child. The boy—Joey—laughed gleefully at Rocco's antics. When he told Rocco to drop it, Rocco complied. Quentin joined in the fun, and soon they were playing "Rocco in the middle" as father and son tossed the ball back and forth over Rocco's head. As soon as Rocco caught on to the game, he began leaping up to catch the ball mid-flight. This made Joey bend over, holding his belly as he laughed with the purest sound she had heard in over ten years.

When Joey began tossing the ball directly to Rocco, Quentin exclaimed, "Hey!" He crouched down and ran over to his son, scooping him up and swinging him around in a circle until they were both dizzy. Savannah found herself smiling as she watched them play. Her fear was still palpable, but the young boy's chortle was a bit contagious, even for a heart as hardened as hers.

As they twirled, Savannah began to see a young Brandon being swung in the same way, by the same guy that was flesh and blood in front of her.

She blinked rapidly, bringing herself back to the present as she tuned in to what was being said to her.

"Go ahead, ask her again." Quentin smiled and rubbed his son's shoulders.

"Please. Stay. For. Lunch!" Joey jumped into the air after each word to punctuate his request.

"Oh, I couldn't..."

"You don't like lunch?" The boy scrunched up his face. "Sometimes I don't like lunch and my dad says, 'You have to eat your lunch.'" Joey deepened his little-boy voice as if imitating his father.

Savannah smiled. "That is true, you do have to eat lunch."

"You could make it for us! Nana Robby isn't here!"

"Joey, she's our guest. We'll make lunch for *her*."

Savannah laughed out loud at the "no way" expression on Joey's face.

Quentin's mouth fell open in mock offense. "Hey, you told me once that I make the best grilled cheese on the planet."

"But not on Mars," the little boy grinned.

"But we're on Earth, so we should be good."

"But she already made food." Joey gestured to the counter.

"But that's for her dog," Quentin sassed back, leaning forward in the same playful way as his son.

The boy placed his little fists on his hips and gave Savannah the exact look his father had given her when she mentioned making the food for Rocco.

"You cooked food for your dog?"

She laughed again. This kid was every bit as much of a character as his father had been when they were younger.

"As a matter of fact, I did."

"But dogs eat trash. And feet."

"They do, do they?" She played along. Obviously his father had taught him something crazy. "Do you have a dog that eats feet?"

The boy giggled. "All dogs eat feet. My teacher brought one to a picnic and it tried to catch everyone's feet to eat them. I wouldn't let it catch me because I'm super fast Joey!" He ran around the kitchen to demonstrate.

"Wow, you sure are fast!"

"All right, all right, you little show-off," Quentin began. "Go wash your hands and get over here to help me put the cheese on the bread. We're going to show this young lady how the Elliot men do things."

"She's not young! She's old. Like you!"

"Ooh, you'd better run, kid." Quentin shrugged at

Savannah as Joey ran away squealing. "I have no control over the things that come out of that kid's mouth."

Savannah felt her heart crackling as she watched the father and son pair playing so joyfully, Rocco following them like the playful pup he was.

Minutes later, Quentin tried to send Joey off to play with his toys while Quentin prepared the bread and cheese, since Joey adamantly refused to participate. Joey ran to Savannah and grabbed her hand. She wanted to jerk away, to recoil from the innocence of his touch. She managed to resist the urge.

"Come with me," Joey demanded.

Savannah looked to Quentin for help. He didn't notice as he busied himself spreading butter on the bread.

Joey pulled.

"I should, ah, I need to help your dad."

"No. He's big. You come see my toys."

Since the buffoon standing next to her wasn't rescuing her from his son, and even Rocco was sprawled across a sunny spot near the window, she had to follow the boy.

She knew she should run. She should come up with some reason why she had to make a sudden departure. This boy didn't know she was a danger. He didn't know she couldn't keep him safe.

He didn't know.

And yet, he wanted her to play. With him. He was the open-eyed, cute-demanding, framed-on-the-wall picture of trust. She couldn't shatter that trust by denying his wishes. Just a few minutes to suffer through, for the sake of the young child's ego, and she could return to her solitary, safe life.

Surely a few moments wouldn't do any harm.

Savannah allowed herself to be dragged to the other room. Joey dumped a box of cardboard blocks and asked her to help him build a tower. She complied, silent at first. He chattered enough for both of them. She focused mainly on the construction activity, but she couldn't help sneaking the occasional peek at the boy. His brown hair was floppy. He had a habit of pushing it out of his eyes with both hands. When he concentrated, his fingers danced as though he were a conductor. He loved to jump and bounce and leap—even if it meant knocking over the tower they were building.

He caught her staring and stared back.

"Are you Daddy's girlfriend?"

She laughed, and though she rarely blushed, she thought she was indeed turning red.

"Oh, no! Not at all."

"Then why are you here? And so pretty?"

She quirked her brow at his seemingly random thoughts.

"You think I'm pretty?"

He nodded.

"If you're not Daddy's girlfriend, you will be mine."

"Is that right?"

"Yup!" He kicked the blocks out of the way. "I was going to have my teacher for a girlfriend but she's getting married. Are you getting married?"

Never. But this wasn't a therapy session.

"Nah, I'm free. I have to tell you, though. I'm not really girlfriend material."

"What?" He tilted his head to the side, trying to figure out the strangeness of the woman before him. "Let's play with Legos."

The tension returned to her body. Of all the toys in the universe, why the ones that most reminded her of her brother?

"Hey, Joey! Food will be ready in five minutes. Start cleaning up." Quentin's shout from the kitchen was perfectly timed.

"Oops, we've got to clean up. No Legos for today."

Joey crossed his arms over his chest, his lip jutting out in a fantastic pout.

"I want you to see what I made." His sock-clad foot stomped with as much vigor as a judge's gavel.

She didn't want to. She *really* didn't want to. But this young replica of Quentin had some strange pull on feelings long buried, and she couldn't fathom disappointing the kid.

She'd have to suck it up.

"Okay, let's toss these quickly into the bucket and then you can show me before we eat. That grilled cheese smells delicious."

Joey did more bouncing around than cleaning, but Savannah didn't mind doing the bulk of it. She was surprised at how easy this felt when she allowed herself to not *think*.

Joey grabbed her hand again, and this time, she

Not Over You

allowed her fingers to relax around his small, chubby hand. She closed her eyes, transported to a time when Brandon had looked up to her. When she was infallible, capable of no harm. When he would hug her and sit on her lap and beg her to read one more story. As a teen, she was most often annoyed at his interference in her life, but they did share those precious moments when she was his world and he was hers. He was always sliding hand-drawn pictures under her door. Many of them were of trophies or rainbows or tree houses (his favorite). The common factor in all of the drawings was the block-style letters spelling out "#1 Sister."

"Look! I'm building a tree house!" Joey's young, squeaky voice startled her back to Quentin's home, where she had been led into a small room lined with bookshelves. Boxes of Legos lined the lower shelves, reminding her of Brandon's room.

Why a tree house? Of all things.

"Come see!" Joey dragged her down to the floor.

"That's impressive," she managed.

"I'm trying to make it as good as that one, but Daddy hasn't been helping like he's 'sposed to."

Savannah gasped when she followed the direction Joey pointed in. No way. No freaking way.

What the hell was Brandon's tree house model doing here? That was his most prized possession. He had been working on it day and night before he died. In fact, he hadn't even wanted to go to the lake that day, but Mother Dearest had said he had to get out; that locking himself in his room day in and day out wasn't healthy for an eight-year-old kid.

She had made him go with Savannah. He never came home.

Savannah backed out of the room. She thought she heard Joey calling out to her, but she couldn't respond. She couldn't even blink. Shock drove all the blood out of her extremities, making her hands cold and her feet feel like they couldn't carry her.

Quentin's hands on her back surprised her.

"Everything okay?"

No. No! Nothing was okay.

"You have Brandon's Legos."

Quentin closed his eyes for a brief second and took a deep breath, dropping his hands away from her as she swung around to confront him.

"Why do you have Brandon's Legos?"

Anger flooded her face and body with fiery heat.

"Answer me." She thought she was keeping her voice in control, not wanting to frighten the child, but she couldn't be sure.

"Joey, go on into the kitchen and see if you can reach your plate from the cabinet."

"I'm out of here." Savannah stormed toward the kitchen, nearly beating Joey there, but Quentin grabbed her arm.

"Why are you so mad?"

"Why am I so mad?" She thought there was a very real possibility that her widening eyes would pop out of her head. "You have my dead brother's most prized possession, the one thing he loved the most in the world, and you are wondering why I'm mad?"

Not Over You

"Peaches," he began.

"Don't you dare call me that."

He took a step closer and held his hands up in surrender. "Savannah, you can have it if you want. Your mother gave me his Legos when Joey was born. She wanted them to be loved by someone else."

Her mother gave them away?

Savannah clenched her fists, driving her fingernails into her palms.

"I'm sorry I didn't warn you. I'm sure it was a shock to see it in there. Joey isn't allowed to play with the tree house—he can only look at it. He's trying to emulate the design."

Her flame went out with that one gust of wind. A child should enjoy the toys as much as her brother had. It was only fair. Still, she couldn't quell the irritation she felt toward her mother.

Her shoulders slumped forward.

She owed him an apology. Damn, how she hated that.

"I'm sorry. I overreacted." The words were a mumbled mess, but sincere. He graced her with a smile.

"No apology necessary, though I am impressed. I don't remember you being the apologizing type."

She swatted him on the arm. "Don't make me retract it."

"Daaaaaad! Dad's girlfriend! Let's go! I'm hungry!"

"Guess that's our cue." Quentin slung his arm around her shoulder. She liked the weight of it. She liked his scent. She liked his warmth.

She shrugged out of his half-embrace, ducking to release herself from the very arm she wanted around her.

"We'll give him the wrong idea."

"I think he already has an idea." Quentin pulled her close again and kissed the top of her head. Why something so simple made her stomach spin faster than the washer on the spin cycle, she had no idea.

"Joey, you remember her name. Savannah. That's what you need to call her."

Savannah smiled and accepted the golden grilled cheese and sweet potato fries. She watched as Quentin's hands sliced apples, amazed at the changes his body had undergone over the years. He had always been well-built and confident, but the past decade had filled him out and roughened his edges in ways she wouldn't have known to fantasize about.

She cleared her thoughts as she reminded herself they were in mixed company. Besides, he may flirt with her now and then, but he had made his intentions known last night when he rejected her advances.

Fine with her. She didn't need the complications.

The next hour passed in a tumbling, dizzying, somewhat-wonderful blur. Watching Quentin with his son brought about a whole different set of fantasies—ones where she played the starring role as the woman of the house. As soon as those thoughts were entertained, she squashed them under her running shoes and began planning her departure. Rocco needed a run and she needed fresh, un-Quentin-ified air.

She said her goodbyes to Joey, who seemed completely uninterested in her as he tried to engage Rocco in another game. Rocco had reached his limit and gave her the "I want to go to sleep now" puppy eyes.

Joey then begged his father for some TV time. Quentin got him set up in the living room while Savannah gathered her dog food, the extra supplies, and slipped her shoes back on.

Quentin offered to help carry her bags out to the car. She tried to decline, but he insisted that he was teaching his son to be a gentleman. How could she deny him when he winked at her that way?

The walk down the front steps and to the driveway was silent. Not having Joey for a buffer was dangerous—she could only think of Quentin's arms and his shoulders and his sweetness. She didn't need it. She didn't want it. Why couldn't she just believe her stinking lies?

And why couldn't he walk in front of her so she could gawk at his well-shaped ass? Mrs. Reynolds was not wrong about that little detail...

She did get to sneak a peek as he loaded her bags and Rocco into the back seat. He caught her gaping when he turned. He leaned against the driver's door, blocking her from escaping. Her heart pounded.

She couldn't do this. Not now. Not ever.

But oh, how she wanted to.

"Don't be a stranger, okay, Peaches?" He brushed the back of his hand against her cheek. She caught herself closing her eyes and sighing for the briefest second before she jumped back, burned by his touch.

"Quentin, you know I'm only here for a short time. I have the appointment next week, then I'm back to my regular life." The look in his eyes couldn't possibly be regret. Or sadness. "I'm sure I'll see you around."

"That's not good enough." He pulled her to him, their hips perfectly aligned as he slouched against the car. "I want to see you on purpose."

Would his eyes always hold this hypnotic power over her? Ten years had passed. Ten freaking years. Their attraction did not feel like one that had been dormant for a decade. It felt as new as the dew she ran through in the morning. As new as the running shoes she bought last month. As new as the organic lettuce on Mondays at the local grocer.

The sound of little feet pounding down the steps and over the gravel interrupted the discussion, causing Quentin to release the hold he had on her hips and her to jump backward as if caught robbing a bank.

She turned to see Joey's bright smile—so like his dad's. He leaped forward, nearly knocking her into Quentin in the process.

She righted herself and tried to ignore the boy's arms around her waist. With nowhere to put her hands, she rested them on the back of his shoulders. She'd love to give him the affection he was looking for, but all she could think of was Brandon's cold, lifeless body lying on the beach. How she had hugged him, desperate to hear a heartbeat. Her screams landing in her own ears as she begged him to breathe, pleaded with him to be playing a sick prank. The horror of being dragged away by someone—she never knew who—as she kicked and screamed and scratched. How she had been held back as they loaded him into an ambulance, the sirens wailing along with her as they drove away.

The last time she had touched a child was when her brother had been pulled from the water, lifeless. On her watch.

"Will you? Will you? Will you? Will you? Will you?"

"Enough, Joey. Go in the house. I'll be there in a minute." Quentin pulled Joey off Savannah's frozen body. Savannah tuned in, shaking her head to clear the fog of memories and pain and regret.

Joey had asked her something. What was it?

The young boy looked crushed. Did she do that to him? She hadn't meant to hurt him. Then again, she never really *meant* to hurt people, yet it happened around her all the time.

She looked at Quentin quizzically. She couldn't form words, so she hoped he could read her mind.

"Joey was asking you to join our ice cream/movie night. It's very informal. He gets to stay up until eight and pick whatever flavor he wants. He doesn't usually invite anyone to come, so I hope you feel special." Quentin smiled in a way that made her feel like he was tiptoeing around her feelings. He was gentle, coaxing, soothing. Could he see her pain?

She coughed a little, trying to dislodge the lump in her throat.

"Pleasepleasepleasepleasepleaseplease—"

"Joey, enough."

"Pleasepleaseplease—"

Savannah could see Quentin getting irritated, though he did a good job of holding back any harsh words. He had definitely perfected the "dad" look, as she could guess that his next words would be corrective and firm.

"I don't know if I can make it, but thanks for inviting me." That was the best she could do. Why couldn't she think of some preexisting plans?

"Daddy, how many days until Friday?"

Quentin started singing the days-of-the-week song, stopping for Joey to finish it. Joey counted the days on his fingers as he sang along.

"Two days! Two days until ice cream. Woohoo!" Joey ran around like an airplane, arms extended wide. "Will you bring sprinkles?" Big brown eyes bore into her dead soul, and she couldn't muster up the strength to tell the kid no.

"I'll try." Defeated by a—what?—six-year-old? "How old are you, anyway?"

"Six!" He ran up the stairs and slammed the front door closed behind him.

"Guess he's done with us, huh?"

Quentin smiled, shaking his head. "We're still working on manners."

"Well with you for a teacher…" Savannah allowed her voice to trail off as she gestured toward her car door. "If you'll excuse me, I think my poor dog has waited long enough."

"I will excuse you, but proper manners dictate an appropriate expression of gratitude for providing a meal."

"You made grilled cheese," she deadpanned.

"Have you ever had a better grilled cheese?" His eyebrows shot up. Cocky bastard.

"As a matter of fact," she really couldn't lie, "No. That was a darned good sandwich." Her stomach flipped again at the thought that neither of them were talking exclusively about the food.

He calmed her nerves. When she was with him, even like this, she could forget for minutes at a time the fear and sadness she carried with her. When she wasn't with him, she remembered that he was complicit in what happened to her brother. She was the responsible party, but if she hadn't been so distracted by his charm and appeal, her brother would still be here today.

She stiffened and shouldered her way past him. He moved, all traces of playfulness gone. When she started to close the door, desperate for a quick escape, he maneuvered his body to prevent the closure.

"So shall I set aside an extra bowl on Friday night?"

Savannah stared ahead, through the bug-streaked windshield to the copse of trees next to the house. She turned the key, waking the engine. "I'll do my best."

"I'll let Joey know."

He backed up, and she backed out, kicking up sand and gravel as she tore out of the driveway and out to the open road.

Chapter Six

Quentin didn't bother to knock. She wouldn't have heard him over the loud 80s rock she was blasting, anyway. He smiled sympathetically at Rocco. The poor beast curled up on the porch, distancing himself from the noise.

Fresh paint assailed his senses as he followed the sound of her singing. He knew she was likely to kill him for sneaking up on her, but he couldn't resist the urge to watch her.

Clad as she was in only a striped button-down shirt (one of her mother's smocks, he guessed), he was gifted with the perfect opportunity to admire her bare legs as she worked. Definitely the legs of a runner. As she reached up to paint the top of the doorframe, the shirt rose dangerously high. His blood rushed at the glimpse of black lace panties. Her bare heel danced up and down to the beat of the music. She bent to dip her brush in the paint, and he had to stop himself from closing the distance between them. Her head began to thrash at the chorus of the song, and he smiled as her hair streaked across the newly painted frame. She didn't seem to notice as she resumed her painting, her singing loud and carefree.

He considered sneaking back out, suddenly awash with guilt for intruding on this private moment. His legs refused to carry him away.

Lost in the sheer beauty of Savannah in this unguarded moment, Quentin didn't register Rocco bolting into the room. Savannah bent toward the dog's face, singing to him. Quentin smiled. The essence of who she was hadn't been altered in spite of the walls she built around herself. In private, she was apparently still the teenage girl who liked to roll down the windows and blast the music and dangle her bare feet into the wind as he cruised down the highway.

Rocco stared at Quentin, and he became nervous that the dog was about to give him away. Sure enough, Savannah turned in his direction, screaming and jumping and knocking the giant CD player to the floor in her effort to turn off the music. Her paintbrush flung from her hands, bounced off the dog, and landed on the hardwood floor.

Torn between amusement and the distinct realization that he was an ass, Quentin rushed forward to pick up the ancient boom box and the brush. She didn't look pleased at his assistance.

"What the hell do you think you're doing?" She brushed her hair away from her face, leaving a pale yellow streak across her forehead. "You don't just sneak up on someone like that." She muttered some expletives and paced the area, her hand on her heart.

"I knocked, but you didn't hear me over the

music," he lied.

"Then you go away! You don't just let yourself in."

"And miss the performance?"

She didn't find him amusing. She reached behind her to a vase full of paintbrushes and chose the largest one to fling at him. It missed him and crashed to the floor.

He smiled. "Missed me."

She roared and fisted her hands. He raised an eyebrow and leaned back. Right against her freshly painted trim.

She burst into laughter.

"That, my dear, is karma." She narrowed her eyes at him as he tried to wipe away the paint with a cloth he had retrieved from the floor. "Don't sneak up on me like that again, you jerk."

He shook his head at his stupidity. She distracted him in ways he wasn't accustomed to.

"I think I've paid my penance."

"I think not." She crept toward him, a tiger stalking her prey. "Not yet."

She closed in on him, and his body picked up where it had been while he was spying on her. He should have been embarrassed about how easily she affected him, but all he could concentrate on was the way her hips flirted with the fabric of the shirt as she walked. How the bottom, below the buttons, opened with every step, teasing him with a peek of her creamy thighs. She didn't stop until her breasts were pressed firmly against his chest. She looked up at him with seductive eyes. His hands moved to her hips, including the hand that still held the paintbrush. Her heat burned him through the shirt. If this was his penance, he'd be a bad boy more often.

Savannah traced the collar of his t-shirt with one graceful index finger, while resting her other hand on his bicep. He swallowed as her finger traced a path over his chest, then back up to his shoulder. His mouth watered for a kiss, but he'd let her toy with him for a moment before taking control.

Her finger trailed down his arm, and she smiled when he inadvertently tensed his muscles. He lowered his head as her finger crept down his hand.

This time he wouldn't tell her no. If he didn't have her soon, he'd combust.

She raised her face to meet his. They were millimeters apart. He could smell the mint gum on her breath.

She removed the paintbrush from his hand, allowing him to fully grasp her hips and pull her as close as they could be with clothes on. And then she broke the spell with vicious laughter as she painted the side of his face.

He had no words. He feigned annoyance at her betrayal, but his heart swelled at her playfulness.

"I see how it is." He wiped his face with the back of his hand. "You should know, this isn't my color."

Her laugh became a snort. Boy, was she proud of herself. He smiled along with her, stifling the urge to laugh out loud as she wrapped her arms around her belly and bent forward, giving in completely to her laughing fit.

He had wondered if they'd ever play again.

He tossed the brush into the paint tray, and then took the lead as predator. Her eyes widened as he twisted around so she was cornered. His hands found the warm place on her hips and he guided her away from the wet paint. Pushed against the wall, she arched her back, driving herself into him. His bulging zipper pressed against her warmth, begging for personal contact. She bent one knee and raised it up to the side of his hip while he helped her stay balanced. Her arms found their way around his neck. She licked her bottom lip before nibbling on it, and he growled as he finally claimed her mouth as his own.

Holy shit. There were no words to describe the pain he was in. The perfection she offered. The fucking pleasure of having her so close to him after all this time.

So much wasted time.

Her fervor matched his. He had felt drawn to women before, but never had he experienced the uncontrollable lust and irresistible attraction he had when around her. He had wondered over the years if his memory of her was a fluke. A dramatized history of teen passion.

She was living, breathing proof that his memories hadn't lied.

His hand moved to her thigh, then upward, pushing the pesky shirt up to grant him access to what he wanted more than anything.

He toyed with the elastic band of her panties, drawing in a breath as her tongue did something wild to his. She pulled his head closer, deepening the kiss. He plunged a finger inside her, nearly exploding when she exclaimed her pleasure into his mouth. Their tongues matched the thrusting of his fingers, and he smiled against her lips as he felt her tense in pleasure.

She reached for his zipper, and though he desperately, *painfully* wanted her to touch him, he knew this day had to be all about her.

He lifted her into his arms. She weighed nothing, but hot damn, did her ass feel good as it bounced against him. He carried her to the bed. She didn't protest.

Her eyes never left his as he slipped her panties down her legs, his kisses trailing behind them. He reached up under the shirt to access her gorgeous breasts. He toyed with her nipples while she writhed against him. Needing an unobstructed view, he slowly unbuttoned her shirt. Her gaze was intense, full of longing. He breathed in the musky perfume of her desire. He wanted to enjoy every second of this act he had spent the last decade dreaming about, yet he felt like an overeager sixteen-year-old, ready to explode if her fingers even grazed him.

Hell, he'd probably come if she so much as looked at his erection.

One whispered word from her and he nearly tossed aside all of his self-control.

"Please."

He closed his eyes, willing himself to maintain control. His mouth took the lead, kissing a trail back down her belly, burying his face in her dark curls. His tongue traced a line down her center, amazed at how she could taste the same after all these years. She was flawless. Perfect. Delicious.

He held her in place as he plunged his tongue into her, increasing the pace as she lifted her hips, forcing him deeper and deeper. He sucked on her swollen clit as he plunged his fingers deep inside her, increasing his rhythm until she screamed out his name.

He struggled to maintain control.

She was too fucking hot.

He was going to combust.

She shouted his name over and over, and the repetition of his name on her lips, and his tongue on her other lips, made his heart and dick swell several sizes.

At her screams, her damned dog jumped onto the bed, interrupting a perfectly wonderful orgasm.

He tried to push the dog away, but the animal growled, baring his teeth. He hadn't seen this side of her beloved pooch yet. Savannah wiped sweat from her forehead and seemed like she was trying to say something. He smiled, happy with the delirious state she was in.

Rocco planted himself across her belly, blocking Quentin's view of Savannah. She laughed and stroked Rocco's head. Quentin sat up and mumbled to himself.

"Where are you going? We're not done here." Her voice was sultry, inviting.

Too sultry. Too inviting.

He shuffled his way to the bathroom, unable to speak. His blood still raced; his thoughts out of control.

He wanted to be inside her more than anything, but he had to wait until the timing was right. For now, cold water splashed on his face would have to suffice.

He spent longer in the bathroom than intended, but his raging boner took forever to go down. Every thought he tried to distract himself with led him back to Savannah. The weight of her breasts in his hands. Her smooth skin at his fingertips. Her soft...

He filled the sink with cold water and stuck his face in until he couldn't hold his breath any longer.

Music lured him out of the bathroom, wiping his face with a ragged towel as he emerged. The music was softer this time, not the raging heavy metal she had been painting to. He didn't recognize the band, but the beat was calm, soothing. There was nothing soothing about the way her hips moved in time to the music as she resumed her painting, though.

After one more face dunk, he felt ready to be in the same room as her.

Rocco lifted his head and glared at him as he approached. Savannah ignored him. Her shirt was buttoned up again, but he didn't miss the fact that her panties remained on the floor. He bit the inside of his cheek.

"So," he cleared his throat, embarrassed at how deep and husky his voice came out. "Why are you painting?"

She looked over her shoulder and graced him with a serene smile.

"I'm not used to being idle. I asked Dad if he'd mind, and he thought it would be great. I guess he's planning to sell this old place to get up some money for Mom's care. Figured while I'm stuck here, I'd make myself useful."

Quentin remained quiet. Sell the studio? He had known money was tight for the retired couple, and the mounting medical bills couldn't be making things easy. He wondered if they'd take some help from him or if Rick would frown upon what he'd perceive to be a handout.

If he cashed out a few stocks...

He hated to see Karyn lose this studio. He hadn't grown as close to her as he had to Rick, but he knew that painting on canvas was therapeutic to the woman. Before she became sick, she spent days at a time here, creating a storm of artwork. After Brandon's death and Savannah's disappearance, she hadn't emerged from this place in over a month.

How could Rick even think of selling?

He shook his head and forced himself back to the moment.

"After the bone marrow transplant is done, you're planning on going back?"

"Back home? Of course." She bent to pick up the paint tray, then moved her operation to another doorframe. "As soon as the blood testing is done, actually. I don't know how the time frames work out for the donation and transplant or whatever, but I'm hoping I can just swing into town when they need me."

"Tell me about your life there. In Maine."

"Not much to tell."

He panicked as he watched the walls going back

up around her. "Sure there is. What's your career?"

She laughed. "I wouldn't exactly call it a career. I was seventeen when I moved there. No college degree, not even proof that I finished high school. I got lucky and found a friend. Valentina gave me a job in her little tourist shop and let me crash in a converted garage that's attached to the shop. Over the years, she's allowed me to sell jewelry I've made. And my dog food."

Rocco's head perked up at the mention of food. When nothing was given to him, he went back to sleep.

"Your dog food?"

"Yeah, I sell it."

"Really?"

"Don't act so surprised. A lot of people care what their animals are eating. I always sell out at the Farmer's Market. The local grocery store carries it, too. I've been asked to expand my operation, but I don't have the ability to do so. Yet."

"Impressive." He meant it. She had carved a life for herself completely independently. She found a gift and made it a business. "And what about your love life? Any guys I need to beat down?"

She laughed, but didn't answer.

"My turn to ask questions." Savannah put the brush down and picked up her bottle of water. After a sip, she leaned against a low bookshelf, careful not to knock over the artwork propped on top.

"What's the deal with Joey's mother?"

Damn, she didn't hold back. Straight for the jugular.

"She's not around."

"Why not?"

"Turns out motherhood wasn't for her."

Savannah crinkled her face in confusion. "She didn't know that before she had him?"

"I don't know. We didn't know each other all that well before it happened. Once he was here, she couldn't take the stress. She disappeared here and there, which is why I hired Nana Robby and asked her to live with us. In my line of work, I needed to be able to pick up and go with little notice."

"And this Robby lady still lives with you?"

"Jealous?"

She rolled her eyes and crossed her arms in front of her.

"She does live with us, but she had to go away for the week to take care of her grandchildren in Florida."

"Do you ever hear from the mother?"

"Nope. She called once—about a month after she left. When she heard Joey screaming in the background, she hung up. Never heard another thing."

"I guess he's better off without her." Savannah said the words, but she didn't look like she believed them.

"We do alright. He's my little buddy. Can't imagine life without him. It's a constant battle to remind him that his mother didn't leave because of him, or because he's unworthy in any way. He has a lot of people who love him. Your parents have been great with him."

He wondered if she realized her fist was rubbing

her chest, right over her heart.

"He really took to you. He's always pretty friendly, but he has never invited anyone to ice cream night. That's always daddy/son time."

She turned away, but he didn't miss the clouds streaming across her blue eyes. She resumed painting—back to the first doorframe. Her strokes were bolder, rougher. Her posture stiff, she looked like more like she was exorcising demons from the wood rather than coating it with paint.

"Peaches, I didn't mean to upset you. It's a compliment."

She shook her head. "It's this wood. No matter how much paint I put on these damned knots, they keep showing through." She soaked the brush with more paint than would ever be necessary, dripping it onto the floor as she moved to apply it.

Clearly something more was bothering her. He approached her from behind—cautiously—like he would an injured person in shock. He placed his hand over hers, guiding the brush over the wood to smooth the lumps and bubbles of paint she had carelessly splashed on.

"The knots will always be there." He whispered into her ear, feeling her tense just before she began to relax into his touch. Her warm back leaned against his chest. She allowed him to lead the painting. "That's because the tree never gives up the fight. No matter how much we try to cover it up, pretend it's something else, the tree will always show us a sign of what it's made of, what it is deep down beneath the exterior."

Her head rested against his shoulder. He inhaled her sweet shampoo, moved by the fact that she was letting down her guard. Finally.

"He's better off not knowing me, Quentin."

He felt the rumble of her soft, quiet words more than he heard them, and yet they punctured his heart just the same.

"I hurt people. I'm not fit to be around children."

He kissed the top of her head before gently turning her in his arms. The paintbrush clattered to the floor, but he didn't care. The floor could be cleaned, repaired, burned to ashes. His Savannah, the love of his life, his precious peach, was broken. Scarred. Deeper than he had even realized. And if he couldn't fix her, he had no right to call himself a man.

"I used to think that of myself, too. I beat myself up over and over for what happened to Brandon. I swore it was my fault. I begged the powers-that-be to take me instead."

Savannah tried to pull away, but he wouldn't release her. She had to hear him. He had to get through to her.

"It wasn't my fault, and it wasn't your fault. You can't punish yourself forever."

She clawed at his arms. He held on tight. Rocco stood up and growled, coming to her rescue. Quentin refused to let go. She pounded on his chest, demanding to be released.

He pulled her in tighter, blocking her arms from moving. He wouldn't let her run away this time.

Rocco paced around them, seemingly unsure how

to react.

"Your family needs you. I need you."

Fire burned in her eyes. Her nostrils flared. He could feel the hatred she directed toward him as strongly as if she had plunged a knife into his gut.

What was he doing?

He let her go and watched as she stormed off in a huff. She slipped on a pair of pants and sneakers, tapped her leg with her hand to call Rocco to her, and disappeared into the woods in a sprint.

He stayed behind and cleaned up the mess.

Chapter Seven

Savannah ran. She ran and she ran until her feet burst with blisters and she couldn't even sweat any longer. She ran until her dog with unlimited energy began to slow. She ran until Quentin's gentle touch was a distant memory.

As she approached the center of town, her body refused to run any longer. Slowing to a walk, she led Rocco onto the town common, where she knew they could find public water fountains. She helped Rocco drink from the dog-friendly spigot at the bottom of the fountain, and then splashed her face and neck with the refreshingly cool liquid. She took a drink, never so grateful for water.

Rocco cocked his head expectantly, patiently waiting for directions. She knew it was too soon to return to the studio. After running the ten miles from the studio to town, Rocco would need a break before running back. Since she left without grabbing any money, it looked like they'd be spending some quality time together on the town common.

Not Over You

Savannah liked blending in, being invisible. Her way-too-social dog tended to bring unwanted attention, but most people were in school or work this time of the day, so she should be safe. She hoped no one would complain about the lack of a leash—she had run out without grabbing it.

Not even fifteen minutes had passed and Savannah was already noticed by a pair of townies. Shouldn't they have croaked by now? They had been ancient when she was in high school. She could only imagine how old they were now.

She ducked her head and pretended not to notice the staring and pointing. Rocco followed her to the pond area, where she hoped to find obscurity among the bushes and willows.

Lady Luck obviously hated her.

"Look who we have here." The unmistakable voice of Harvey, one of the ancients who probably lived here when the town was first established hundreds of years ago, greeted her. "I'll be damned."

Grimacing before smiling, Savannah lifted her head in greeting. "Hi, Harvey. Bruce."

The old men, Bruce with his walker, Harvey with his beer can wrapped in an insulated cover, hustled toward her. Rocco moved forward, tail stump wagging, eager to make new friends, until Savannah gave him a quiet command to stay.

"Your mother made no mention that you'd be back," Bruce spat the words through his toothless gums. "If we'da known, we coulda thrown together a welcome home party. You know how the committee loves an excuse for a party."

"Oh, it's temporary. No need for festivities."

"What?" He cupped his hand behind his ear. "These damned hearing aids don't work like they're supposeta. Say that again, darling."

Savannah took a deep breath, praying for some level of patience.

"I'm not here long. No parties."

"Well you didn't haveta shout!" Bruce elbowed Harvey, guffawing at his own non-funny old man humor.

She forced a smile.

"Good to see you gentlemen. I've got to keep moving before my muscles cramp up." Savannah started to move away, but the old men were oblivious to her intentions.

"So where'd you run off to, Savvy girl?" Harvey leaned against a tree, waiting for her to deliver her life story. When she couldn't manage any words, he filled in the silence. "Nothing much has changed around here. We keep battling to keep things the same, while the younger folks keep fighting to change things. Like that there thing—" Harvey gestured to a giant structure on the other side of the pond. Huge sheets of canvas enclosed the monstrosity. She had noticed it when she drove by the common before, but with all the other anxiety, she had forgotten to wonder about it. "Then again, that's for a good cause."

Harvey downed his drink. He belched. She winced.

"That man of yours, he's a good one." Bruce piped in. "No one could believe when that wretched woman left him and his boy like that. Especially after you gone and done the same thing."

She stared at Bruce, shocked at his lack of a filter.

"I didn't mean any offense, close that moutha yours. The guy was heartbroken after everything."

Whatever he said after that, Savannah didn't hear. She mumbled for spite and ran with Rocco out of the common. So much for a respite from the all-consuming chaos surrounding Quentin.

What was with the people of this town? Ten years had passed. *Ten years.* Couldn't they let go of a high school romance? Why did they even care so much? As she could recall, no one had cared too much about Quentin back then. They all thought he had no future. That his parents never should have had him. That he would turn out to be as much of a waste of space as they felt his parents had always been.

Why would they think she'd still be as in love with him now as she had been in high school?

Things changed.

People changed.

They'd just have to accept that.

Savannah roamed through the back streets of Healing Springs, clearly not able to find peace in town. When she felt her body had been punished enough and was finally deplete of emotion, she led Rocco back to her temporary home.

***

Savannah bolted out of bed, sweat dripping down

her temples and between her breasts. She had been tossing and turning with a vivid nightmare. Her brother splashing in the water with his friend. Her brother's friend running to her spot on the beach. Quentin dragging her brother's still body out of the water. The roar of the sirens, the thrust of her fists on her own head, the screaming of her mother at the hospital. Her brother's face smiling at her in a warped reflection.

She pressed her palm to her heart, desperate to calm the thudding. It took her a moment to realize the banging at the door was not part of her nightmare.

She wrapped the sheet around herself and peered out the window next to the door.

What the hell was he doing here? And with the child in his arms?

She shooed Rocco away as she swung the door open.

"I'm sorry to wake you."

"What are you doing here? It's the middle of the night."

"I know. I'm sorry. I'm not supposed to be working, but there was a huge accident and they need all responders. Nana Robby won't be back until tomorrow. There's no one else I can ask."

His eyes begged a question she didn't compute.

Quentin brushed by her and carried his sleeping son to the futon on the other side of the room.

"What are you doing?"

"I'll be back as soon as I can. He won't be any trouble."

Ice ran through her veins, freezing her to the spot.

Rocco must have sensed her fear, as he glued himself to the side of her leg.

"No..." Fear clogged her throat, rendering her unable to defend herself against this imposition. This threat. This horror show.

"I know we didn't leave things in a great place earlier. I'm sorry. But I don't have time to find someone else to watch him."

She grabbed his arm as he tried to leave.

"I can't. You can't leave him here."

Quentin kissed the spot between her eyes. "He'll be sleeping. I'll be back before you know it. Go back to sleep."

No.

How could she sleep? How could she take her attention away from the child? How would she ever live with herself if her negligence caused the death of another sweet soul?

She watched as Quentin ran to his truck. He didn't even look back before zipping out of the driveway, his little red siren spinning on his dashboard.

She'd kill the man.

Joey moaned in his sleep. She jumped back, tightening the sheet over her chest. *Please stay asleep.*

Rocco ran to the child and licked his feet.

"Rocco, down." Rocco stopped mid-lick. "Don't you dare wake him up." Her whisper sounded scratchy to her own ears.

Savannah held her breath as Rocco lifted himself onto the futon, snuggling in near the boy's feet. She glared at the dog, hoping he could sense her irritation.

He gave a defiant glare back, and then tucked his head into the afghan the boy was wrapped in and closed his eyes.

Maybe he knew the kid needed protecting.

Savannah shuffled over to the electric teakettle and prepared water. She'd need caffeine to help her stay alert. Not that she was in any hurry to go back to Nightmareland, anyway.

Tea in hand, Savannah pulled a chair over near the futon. She'd watch the kid, all right. She wouldn't take her eyes off him.

Joey's lashes fanned across his cheeks. In the dim light, she could still make out the few freckles that had formed on his face. His hair was a disheveled mess—not that she could judge. His thumb rested near his mouth, grazing his bottom lip. Was he a thumb sucker? She remembered Brandon having the hardest time quitting his thumb when he was six. Her mother would punish him when she caught him in action, but Savannah made quitting a game. He had been so proud when he kicked the habit. As a reward, Savannah offered to supervise a sleepover for a bunch of his friends.

Joey mumbled something in his sleep, and then flipped over on the futon. His blanket fluttered to the ground. Savannah picked the hand-knit afghan off the floor and gently tucked it around the small boy's frame, shoving Rocco away. She lingered for a moment, her heart swelling as she studied him up close.

Everything about this boy reminded Savannah of

her brother. His knobby little elbows. His dinosaur pajamas. The way he went from fetal position to taking up the entire space with his open legs. The way he breathed—the occasional snore mixed in with sleep-talking in what sounded like another language.

Maybe these were universal boy traits, but for the first time in ten years, Savannah had to blink away a tear. Ashamed, she backed away, returned to her chair, and vowed she'd never let her guard down around a child again.

***

Savannah startled awake as her foot plummeted to the floor. Confused for a moment, she wiped drool from the side of her face and tried to remember where she was.

A tiny, muffled cry had her darting out of her chair. That's right, she was in the studio. In Healing Springs. Babysitting. She was supposed to stay awake to be sure no harm came to Quentin's son, yet she had failed, as she had suspected she would.

She rushed to Joey's side, checking him over for injuries. What could have happened? Rocco shared the same confusion, but his instincts drove him to comfort the boy while Savannah's instincts warned her to run.

But she was the only human here who could help the child.

What was Quentin thinking, leaving Joey here with her?

Her hands shook as she placed them on his back.

He was warm, but not hot. He didn't feel feverish. He rolled over, huddling into a small, tight ball. The blanket fluttered to the floor in a heap of yarn and unraveling dreams.

His cries, muffled by his fists and the back of the futon, grew in intensity. His little body vibrated and shook.

"Joey, honey. Wake up."

She didn't want him to be awake, but she couldn't stand this sadness he was immersed in. She knew too well the pain of a night terror.

When he didn't respond to her gentle prodding, she scooped him up in her arms. He immediately wrapped his arms around her neck, settling his wet face into the curve of her neck.

Now what?

She stayed as still as the statue on the town common as Joey wrapped his fingers into her hair, twirling and tugging.

"Mama."

She stiffened even more.

His tiny voice was more infant-like in his sleep.

His body continued to vibrate as his tears gushed onto her neck and shoulder. She wished she were the sort of person who could offer comfort rather than bring harm.

Rocco tried to insinuate himself onto her lap along with Joey. When would this dog learn that at one hundred ten pounds, he was not a lap dog?

After shooing Rocco away and rewarding him with a "good boy" when he settled in beside her, she closed

Not Over You

her eyes and rested her head on Joey's.

His tears slowed as she breathed on his head. He smelled of watermelon shampoo and bubble bath and dreams.

His innocence must have intoxicated her, because she started singing a long-forgotten lullaby. Her voice crackled as she tried to keep her volume down. His cries stopped and he settled into her arms, resting his still-sleeping head on her chest.

When she reached the second verse of the song, his breathing was steady and slow with no trace of tears.

She smiled as she looked down at this young boy—so trusting in her arms. For a nanosecond, she could almost convince herself that she had done something well tonight. That she hadn't hurt him. That she had maybe even helped him.

And then the ghost she carried around with her screamed at her. She should have called his father. She should have woken him up. She should have done something—anything.

She tried to untangle Joey from her arms, but as her muscles tensed, he clung tighter. There was no way to put him down without waking him up, and he was so incredibly peaceful. Besides, what would she do with him if he were awake?

She settled in with the child, ignoring her cramping legs and sore arms—arms that were unaccustomed to holding a child. She hadn't killed Rocco yet, right? Maybe this would be okay.

Her eyes fluttered closed, but she promised

herself she wouldn't fall asleep. This day had been so incredibly tiring. And Joey's warmth and smell and sweetness had her feeling more relaxed than she could ever remember being.

***

Quentin let himself in when his gentle knock didn't bring Savannah to the door. Her stepfather had given Quentin the key so he could help maintain the property, since he lived so close. Hours had passed since he had dropped Joey off with Savannah, and if he didn't have to wake her again, he wouldn't.

His heart melted as soon as he entered the dimly lit room. A low-watt lamp cast a glow on the most beautiful sight he had ever seen. An image he had dreamed about, but never imagined seeing in reality.

Savannah was asleep, all right, but not in her bed. On the futon, Savannah was blanketed by Joey and Rocco. She couldn't be comfortable, but her eyes remained closed, even as the floor creaked under his weight. He didn't want to disturb this perfect picture, but he didn't want her to be achy.

Kissing Savannah on the head, he gently pried her hands off of Joey. He swung his son into his arms, intending to move him to the side of Savannah. A gasp tore out of Savannah's throat as she jumped at the disturbance.

"What the hell?" she screeched.

"Shh. Go back to sleep. I was just moving Joey so

you'd be more comfortable."

Savannah leapt off the futon, stumbling a bit before righting herself.

"How did you get in? I made sure the door was locked." Her eyes were frantic. She searched the room as if looking for more intruders. Her posture suggested she was ready to fight. Rocco perked up and moved in front of Savannah, sniffing Joey's dangling feet and seeming to challenge Quentin for the right to the child.

"I have a key. Didn't I tell you that?"

"No. No, you didn't." She closed her eyes and pressed her palm to her chest. After a moment of breathing, she graced him with accusatory eyes. "Why do you have a key?"

"That's how neighbors do things around here, Peaches. Have you forgotten the charm of the small town life?" He raised an eyebrow, desperately wishing circumstances were different and he had let himself in for another purpose. If his son weren't here...

No use torturing himself with those thoughts. Given her expression, he didn't stand a chance, anyway.

"Was he okay for you?"

"No. He needed you and you weren't here for him."

Ouch.

"What happened?"

"He cried. He cried and needed comfort and you left him here with the person *least* equipped to help him."

"Kids cry in their sleep sometimes. He was

probably having a nightmare. And clearly my judgment isn't as bad as you're accusing me of, because he is still sound asleep and no worse for the experience."

"He called out for his mother. How the hell am I supposed to help him with that?"

Shit. His mother? He hadn't called out for her in years. Joey had asked questions when he first entered kindergarten in the fall and all the other kids cried for their moms in school, but he seemed to be pretty well adjusted, considering the circumstances. Why had he called out for a woman he didn't know? And tonight, of all nights?

"I'm sorry," Quentin muttered.

Savannah had her hands on her hips, her skin-tight tank top showing all of her attributes. He had to get the hell out of here before he angered her even more.

"Yeah, well don't assume I'm here to be your babysitter. You'd better come up with a Plan B for when your sitter is out of town, because I'm not qualified. Or interested."

He knew that bringing Joey here was a risk, but with lives on the line at that accident site, he thought that pissing Savannah off was the least of his worries. The kid was sleeping, while someone else's kid would probably never walk again. Savannah ran from her problems while someone's wife and mother *died* tonight in that crash.

Yes, she had demons to battle, but at least she was alive and able to battle them.

He wondered how the good doctor who was driving tonight would deal with the fact that he hadn't been able to save his wife and protect his young daughter. If he ever woke from the coma.

Quentin yanked Joey's blanket off the futon, thankful the boy slept so soundly.

"I won't trouble you again."

"Good."

"Good."

He slammed out the door, jostling Joey awake in the process. He changed his energy to a calmer one, though inside his blood continued to roar. Joey looked at him through heavy eyelids as Quentin loaded him into his booster seat, taking extra care to buckle him carefully. The ride was less than a minute, but after what he had seen tonight, he refused to take any chances with his son's safety.

And he'd be damned if he'd go out of his way to see, speak to, or know Savannah Grace. She had made her feelings clear. He would respect them.

Chapter Eight

Three more days. Three more days of this living hell. Three more days until the expedited test results would determine whether or not Savannah was a match for her mother's bone marrow. Three more days until she will have fulfilled her obligation and could return home.

Three more days until she could put this town behind her again.

After another tense visit with her parents, where her dad had forced her to stay for brunch before he'd give her the keys to her newly repaired car, and a rushed blood test with the only doctor her mother trusted in the entire universe, she now felt free to leave Healing Springs for a few hours. Her obligations had been met, and she couldn't sit around and stress about whether she'd deliver another disappointment to her mother.

She felt bad leaving Rocco behind, but like most men she knew, he truly preferred to stay home and laze around. Until society learned to embrace dogs in all facets of culture, Rocco wouldn't be allowed in the mall, anyway.

Though Savannah had never been one for retail therapy, she knew she needed a Friday night fix at the bar tonight, and the only shoes she had brought were sneakers. She needed a pair of slutty heels to get her through this weekend.

With the nearest mall over an hour away, she settled into her seat for a stress-relieving drive.

Was there any freedom quite like the open highway?

She reflected on the upcoming evening, on how desperately she needed to utilize her weekend persona. How much better she'd feel after she applied the temporary salve that came in the form of expensive liquor and cheap sex.

She needed to distance herself from everything that made her *feel*. Feeling led to hurting—herself and others. She had been flirting with emotional disaster every time she allowed herself to grow closer to Quentin. Letting her guard down around that little boy—inexcusable.

The mall was quiet and filled with people she didn't know, which she appreciated. She found the right pair of stilettos almost immediately, splurged on a tight-across-the-chest blouse and a push-up bra, and then found herself, in a trance, walking through a children's toy store.

What was she trying to do to herself?

She pushed all thought out of her mind as she selected a robotic dinosaur toy. She paid for it, bought a gift bag, and refused to acknowledge that she had just purchased a gift for a child she shouldn't be thinking about.

Savannah locked the gift in her trunk, knowing she shouldn't have bought it. She had no intention of seeing Joey or his father. She was going to do what she did best—drown her bad memories with bad decisions.

In the driver's seat, she slipped her heels on her feet, unbuttoned an extra button on her shirt, mussed her hair, blasted the music, and reminded herself of who she really was.

***

The music was loud and, well, *bad*. The bar was almost empty. She had thought that waiting until nine to enter would guarantee a better crowd to blend in with, but clearly she was wrong.

After dropping the gift bag off on Quentin's porch, she had raced back to her house and prepared herself for a shady night out.

She scoped the bar without making her intentions too obvious. Not that she cared who judged— everyone had their ways of coping, and this was hers. She wanted to make her selection carefully before she struck.

The perfect guy was all the way at the other side of the bar, alone. He looked to be about her age, with a handsome face and a decent body. His clothing was small-town-average, like he had lived here all his life and was secure in his situation. He would be content with the level of what she had to offer. She doubted he'd even bother to try to get her number after.

She ordered a shot of tequila, downed it fast, then ordered another. The bartender, unfamiliar to her, smiled as she toyed with the shot glass. His salt-and-pepper hair framed a friendly face, but he didn't attempt to initiate conversation. He served up her drinks, took her payment, and continued down the line.

Like clockwork, her target made eye contact exactly when she predicted he would. He looked over his shoulder, checking to be sure there wasn't someone behind him, as if surprised that she'd be inviting him with her eyes. She'd have to work harder than she liked to on this one.

With a freshly served rum and coke in hand, she maneuvered her way through the increasing crowd of Friday night drinkers until she was three stools away from her target. Up close, he looked vaguely familiar. She hoped she was wrong.

"Weren't you in my bio class? Way back when?" His voice wasn't unpleasant, but it didn't make her belly do trampoline flips like Quentin's did. Good. No fireworks were necessary. She faked a smile and he continued. "Yeah, yeah. You were the one who refused to dissect the rat."

"Got me." She threw up her hands in phony surrender, then downed her drink and gestured for the bartender.

"Let me get that for you." She sat back in her stool, watching as he nearly fell over trying to signal for a refill.

She stared at him as she sipped her drink. The faster she got wasted, the sooner she could kill off the voices haunting her. Quentin's. Brandon's. Joey's.

Screw sipping—she downed the drink in one big gulp.

"Are you here for our ten year reunion?"

"No."

He looked at his hands, wrapped around his sweaty beer glass. His face lit up with sudden realization. She looked away and rolled her eyes before turning back to him.

"Oh, I remember now. You're the one who—"

"You want to spend all night talking?" Annoyance marked her tone, not that he'd probably pick up on it. If he said what she was sure he was going to say, she'd have to start all over with another target.

He shut his mouth and shook his head.

He moved to the next stool, leaning across the corner of the bar in a clumsy attempt to kiss her. She pulled away and downed the last drops of liquid in her glass.

"Let's go." She tossed some cash onto the bar and started to leave as he fumbled with his wallet to pay his tab.

Her limbs were beginning to feel the familiar relaxation a good buzz could bring. She wasn't exactly anticipating what was to come, but if he was even halfway decent, he might help her forget everything for a little while.

His hand on her lower back felt strange, and she

had to stop herself from slapping it away. He had no idea the torment that played like a horror movie in her head. He thought she was looking for a good time, and he was prepared to offer one.

This wasn't her first rodeo. But for some reason, she was having a harder time disconnecting.

Without warning, she stopped in front of the liquor store, grateful they had elected to extend the hours since her high school days when they closed by six.

"Go grab a bottle of whiskey."

He didn't argue, nor did he seem offended at her caustic, demanding tone. They'd both get what they wanted tonight, and he wasn't dumb enough to expect kindness on top of it all.

She paced the area, appreciating the blisters forming on the back of her heels. The new shoes did wonders for distracting her from the emotional pain.

Savannah focused on the click of her heels on the pavement so she could tune out the cheerful sounds of the locals on this warm, late spring night. If the guy didn't hurry the hell up, she just might head home and take care of things herself.

She didn't bother looking when she heard footsteps closing in on her.

"'Bout time." She started walking, not sure where they were heading, but not in the mood to ask.

"Are we in a hurry to get somewhere?"

She stopped short, nearly falling on her face. That was not the pleasant, sort of geeky voice of the guy she picked up in the bar. No, that was the voice of her dreams. And her nightmares. The one who could hypnotize her from across a room. The last person on earth she wanted to run into.

Damn, how she hated small towns.

She whipped around, not sure why she felt so ashamed, but eager to make the feeling go away.

"My bad. I thought you were someone else."

He leaned against the corner of the building, grinning that smug *you-know-you-want-me* grin.

"We missed you tonight."

"I told you I wouldn't be there."

"Yeah, but we hoped. Joey was disappointed."

She glanced down at her shoes before reminding herself that he was the one that put her in the crappy situation. She didn't ask for it. He had no right to make her feel bad.

"That's kind of your fault, wouldn't you say?"

He bristled at her words, visibly tensing before shoving his hands into his pockets.

The world stopped spinning as they stared each other down, frozen in time. Her own world may have been spinning a bit, but she'd be damned if she'd show him her vulnerability.

The guy she had picked up in the bar—the one whose name she hadn't bothered to learn and she certainly couldn't remember from high school—swaggered out of the liquor store with a brown bag in hand.

"Sorry it took so long," the guy said. "They're running some special for parents of graduating seniors. Crazy lines."

Graduating seniors. He might as well have punched her in the gut.

Brandon would have graduated this year. Why had that not occurred to her? She had ignored the signs—the school colors decorating the town, the band practicing late in the afternoons, the landscaping being done on the part of the common where they typically held the ceremony.

Nameless guy suddenly noticed they weren't alone. He cleared his throat, looking between Savannah and Quentin as if trying to decide whether he should run or stand his ground.

Quentin stood to his full height, which was a good six inches taller than the guy she had picked up. She doubted he intended to be intimidating, but the other guy took a step back. She rolled her eyes.

"Heyyyyyyyy!" A squeaky, intoxicated voice drew everyone's attention to a wobbly blonde, who hobbled over their way. She stumbled into Savannah before falling into Quentin's arms, her too-skinny arms wrapped around his neck. "Where you been, you bad boy? I thought you'd call."

Savannah watched as Quentin's face became flushed.

So she wasn't the only one playing the field.

"You're drunk." Quentin stated the obvious, holding the blonde at arm's length as she pouted and blinked her heavy eyelashes.

"Drunk for you. What're you up to tonight? Feel like taking me home?" She didn't sound nearly as sultry as she tried to. Not with every other word slurring. "We can go to my place again."

Savannah wanted to leave, she really did, and with Quentin occupied, she had the perfect opportunity to escape. Only problem was that this scene was far too captivating to convince her feet to carry her away.

Even the guy she had picked up seemed drawn into the drama.

Before Quentin could respond to the drunk girl's invitation, a gaggle of her friends hooted from across the street.

"Yo, Ari. Get your drunk ass over here. We've got the Jell-o shots!"

"Jell-o shots!" The girl squealed. "Come with me, Q-Q. Please?"

Quentin shook his head. "You go on without me."

"You're a meanie."

Savannah wanted to rip that pouty lip off the pretty girl's face and slap her with it. Had she no pride?

"Go on—your friends are waiting for you."

"Promise you'll call me soon?"

Quentin didn't answer, but Ari lifted herself up on her tiptoes to kiss him. He moved his head in time for her lips to land on his cheek. Drunk as a marinated cherry, she didn't seem to notice. She laughed at herself as she ran across the street, shouting for her friends to wait up.

"Ari, huh? Isn't she the underclassman who was always trying to break us up in high school? So cute that she finally got you to date her."

"We're not dating."

"Hmm, that's not what she seems to think. If you

Not Over You

hurry, you can catch up to her."

"That's not what I want, and you damn well know it." His lips were set in a firm line, betraying his irritation.

"See you around, Quentin. Or is it 'Q-Q'?" She grabbed what's-his-name's arm and started to move away.

"Really, Savannah? This is the game you're playing?" His voice was calm, tense. Deadly. Not at all the laid back, gentle, encouraging guy he had been since she crashed into him several days ago.

"No game. Just living my life." She leaned into her guy-prop. She could nearly smell the fear on him.

"What you're doing isn't living." Quentin stepped forward and put his hand on the guy's shoulder. Stupid guy tensed. "Good luck with this one, Nick."

And then he walked away.

Nick shrugged his shoulder where Quentin's hand had just been. He looked around, almost as if trying to figure out what strange thing would happen next. He turned back to her, a quizzical look on his face.

"You used to date him? In high school?"

Disgusted, Savannah grabbed the brown bag encased bottle out of his hands. "Go to hell."

She stormed off, wanting to guzzle the contents in one giant sip, but knowing she'd need to get herself home first. Since she had allowed herself too many drinks to drive, she'd have to huff her way back to the studio. All ten miles.

She suddenly hated her new heels.

She heard Nick calling out to her, exasperation

lending an edge to his voice, but she didn't give two sticks about his deflated ego or unfulfilled expectations. To hell with men. To hell with this town. To hell with dealing with problems the way she saw fit. To hell with herself.

She didn't know what she'd do with the rest of her night, but she was grateful to see Nick had splurged for the good stuff.

***

Quentin stormed around town for a full thirty minutes before being able to remember where he had parked his car. His focus was too wrapped up in his heart-stopping encounter with Savannah.

He had sworn just last night that he wouldn't even think about her anymore, yet when he had run into her in town, he had allowed himself to imagine that she'd be happy to see him; that they could put aside the spat they had and move forward. He could never stay angry with her. This time, though…

Quentin wasn't a violent man, but he had to resist the urge to pummel Nick. Not that the guy did anything knowingly wrong. But that didn't stop the ire from running through Quentin's veins at the thought of anyone touching his Savannah. His Peach. His love.

Some love. Obviously she had no problem getting over Quentin.

He had been able to smell the alcohol on

Savannah, but he knew she was fully in charge of herself. She wasn't being taken advantage of—she was taking advantage.

That poor fool had no idea that he was going to be chewed up and spit out.

What the hell was she thinking?

He cursed as he punched the brick wall. Stupidly, he had allowed himself to think she had feelings for him still. That he could help her heal from the pain of the past and they could pick up where they had left off ten years ago.

Clearly he was an idiot.

He clenched his fists, ignoring the pain of his rapidly swelling knuckles.

She did the worst things to him. And the greatest things, too.

The look in her eyes when that other guy came out of the liquor store betrayed her outer confidence. She was ashamed to be caught in the act. When Quentin had hinted about her missing ice cream night with Joey, she had flinched before hardening her expression.

That must mean something, right?

As his red rage faded to a calmer orange, and a light, cleansing rain began misting around him, he realized he was even more of an idiot than he had thought.

He couldn't simply discount the fact that coming back to Healing Springs was more than likely triggering pain she had buried years ago. She had fled immediately after the death of her brother—before she even accepted her high school diploma. She had isolated herself from everyone, and had only agreed to come back here because her mother's life was on the line and she hoped to be a match for the bone marrow donation.

Even still, she had kept her distance from everyone in town, including her family.

And then he had forced her to watch his kid. Before she was ready. When she still hadn't forgiven herself for what had happened when she was a teenager.

Damn it all to hell!

He screwed up. Big time.

She was doing what she had to do to chase away the pain. Hadn't he been in that position, too? Isn't that how he got involved with Joey's mother in the first place?

When Quentin had tracked Savannah down in her new town, he had foolishly thought he'd be able to convince her that she should return home. All through high school and college, he had worked his ass off and invested all of his earnings—every penny that he didn't need to support himself. His intention had always been to make a good life for them, and that didn't change just because she had disappeared. Once he had a good nest egg, he bought the house she always wanted. He worked tirelessly to fix it up, to make it a place she could feel safe and secure and loved.

When he went to her town, he hadn't been able to get close to her. He saw her from a distance, reorganizing a shelf. He could feel her pain all the way across the store. It crippled him. It made him realize he had no business trying to save someone else when he had failed her brother so miserably.

That's when he made the decision to toss aside his business degree and pursue a career as a paramedic. He couldn't change the past, but he could commit to saving as many people as possible.

He had convinced himself that as soon as he had redeemed himself, he'd come back for her.

Lost in his own pain, he had allowed himself to get dragged into a pseudo-relationship with Merry, who turned out to be anything *but* merry when she realized he'd never love her the way he loved Savannah. He tried to do right by her when they found out she was pregnant with Joey—he even tried his best to be happy with this unexpected path—but she never bought his act and decided this life wasn't the right one for her, anyway.

He had no regrets, because he loved his boy more than anything in the world.

He just wished he could fix the future.

With his new insight, he wanted to kick himself in the ass for storming away from her. He should have done something. He shouldn't have left her with her pain. He shouldn't have let her down.

On his way to his car, Quentin noticed that Ari and her group were still going strong in the common. He was surprised the police hadn't asked them to move along, but since tourist season wasn't in full swing yet, they only had one or two officers on duty at any given moment. And the light rain that had fallen eased up immediately, almost like he had imagined it.

He averted his eyes from the group, not wanting Ari to notice him. A male voice rose about the giggles, and he couldn't help but recognize the voice of Nick, the guy who had been with Savannah.

He moved away from the streetlight and studied the crowd, searching for a sign that Savannah was okay. He didn't see her as the party-crowd type—she was too much of a loner—but maybe he was wrong. Or maybe she made an exception tonight.

Nick had three women draped on him and a can of whipped cream being emptied onto his laughing face. Savannah was not one of the participants.

He scanned the street and immediately found her car parked a few spaces away from his.

He jogged toward her car. She wasn't in it.

"Hey," Quentin called over the fence to Nick. The gals started squealing when they noticed Quentin. He shoved his hands into his pockets and stood his ground. The fence would keep them away. Nick's smile faded when he met Quentin's eyes.

"Haven't you done enough to ruin my night?"

"Where is she?" Quentin didn't recognize the lethality in his own voice. He couldn't remember a time when he felt more protective.

Nick ignored him, turning back to the women.

Quentin walked around to the entrance of the common. One scathing look at Ari and her friends and they backed away as fast as they had swarmed him. Nick huffed himself up, getting braver with his alcohol consumption, apparently.

"Jesus, what do you want?" Nick spouted.

"Where is she?" Quentin moved closer, his hands curling into tight fists.

"Calm yourself, dude. That dick tease is long gone. Took my whiskey and ran off before even coming close to sealing the deal." Nick draped his arms over the shoulders of two women. They laughed and joked with one another as they sucked down red Jell-o shots from a plastic cup. "But it's all good. Her replacements are far more interesting to me."

He itched to punch the cocky SOB in the mouth to shut him up. He managed to restrain himself, though he did step closer. The women wiggled their way out of Nick's grasp, probably sensing the threat of aggression.

"If I hear one more negative word about her, you'd better pray for mercy."

Nick looked around, nervously licking his lips and twitching his head.

Quentin glared at him for a good long while before heading back to his car. Though hitting Nick may have offered temporary relief, it was far more important for him to find Savannah.

Most businesses were closed, but he searched the few that were still open. No sign of Savannah.

Driving to her studio, his heart accelerated nearly as fast as his car. Would she have walked home? She had been under the influence, so maybe she didn't want to take any risks. Smart girl.

Except now the off and on, misting rain was erupting into a downpour. He hoped someone had picked her up and given her a ride. Though the air temperature was warm, the rain would quickly cool things down.

Rocco greeted him when he opened the door. The animal paced back and forth on the porch, and Quentin knew the dog was as worried about Savannah as he was. He hadn't passed her on the way here. He was sure of it. He couldn't imagine she'd have drifted off into the woods in the shoes she had been wearing.

He didn't know why, but his gut told him where he could find her.

Rocco ran alongside him as Quentin booked it down to the lake. Quite honestly, he wasn't sure who was leading whom.

He slowed to catch his breath as soon as he saw her. She was huddled in the sand, curled up in a ball. Rain soaked her, but she remained still. Rocco ran to her, licking her cheek and causing her to roll over, shielding her face from his giant tongue. Quentin released a breath he hadn't realized he had been holding. She was okay.

As soon as he was within fifteen feet, he noticed the whiskey bottle on the ground beside her. He kicked it, surprised to see it empty.

She mumbled something, but was slurring too badly for him to make any sense of what she was saying.

Without a second thought, he swung her into his arms and carried her back to the studio. He considered bringing her to his house, but figured he was already on her shit list for everything else.

Once he got her settled in dry clothes and the

Not Over You

warm bed, Quentin sent a message to Nana Robby letting her know he'd be staying out for the night.

No way was he leaving her in this condition. He didn't care what battle would ensue in the morning— he would remain by her side until he knew she was safe.

Chapter Nine

Savannah stretched her limbs, rotating her feet to ease the soreness in her ankles. As soon as she opened her eyes, she regretted the decision. Her hands immediately covered her face to protect her from the blasted sunlight streaming in. Her mouth was dry, gritty.

Wait a minute.

How did she get to her bed?

She sat upright, struggling to make sense of last night.

Her hair felt heavy, slightly damp underneath and full of... sand. She was in her pajamas, but still wearing her bra. Usually the bra was the first thing off, so why did she leave it on? And usually she didn't even bother with PJs when she was as rip-roaring drunk as she had been last night.

She stumbled out of the bed, tripping over Rocco. He lifted his head and groaned, annoyed at the disruption. She stuck her tongue out at him and continued to the bathroom.

She passed the strange man on the futon, closed the bathroom door, and then whipped it open again.

Strange man on the futon?

She doubled back, trying to be stealthy, but sounding more like a hippo ballerina on crack as she struggled to maintain her balance. She leaned down and peered over the wide male shoulders, steadying herself on the wooden arm of the futon.

Okay, not so strange. Quentin.

But what was he doing here?

She squinted as she played back the previous night in her head. The encounter with Nick and Quentin. Her walking halfway home before accepting a ride from an old teacher she could recognize but not recall. Stumbling down to the beach, determined to face her fears. Falling into the bottle of whiskey and playing Mind Eraser. Alone.

So where did Quentin fit into the latter part of this equation?

How did he find her? And why did he stay?

She hurried into the bathroom. Her dry mouth appreciated the brushing and the mouthwash. She tried to comb through her hair with her fingers, but the combination of sleeping on it while it was wet and apparently bringing half the beach home in it made brushing impossible.

She'd have to take a quick shower. No way did she want Quentin to see her like this.

The hot shower (thanks to her stepdad sending Quentin to fix it days ago) helped ease away the hangover she thought she might struggle with. She didn't normally suffer the day after a night out, but she also usually stopped well before she had last night.

She wrapped herself in a towel and hummed as she selected her clothes. Quentin remained asleep. Rocco, too.

Since she couldn't recall what happened last night, she had to assume that Quentin had found her—passed out—on the beach, brought her home, and stayed to watch out for her.

She supposed that meant he earned a cup of coffee when he awoke. Hell, she needed one, too.

She started the coffee pot and whipped up a batch of "microwave muffins in a mug." She'd be extra kind and make him breakfast before kicking him to the curb.

When the coffee was done, she carried her mug over to the chair near the futon where she had watched over Joey a short time ago. Rocco stood within reach of her extended foot, waiting expectantly for a rubbing. She obliged, inhaling the coffee aroma and staring at Quentin.

Even sleeping, the man looked amazing. He had matured as he aged, but he hadn't really changed. He rolled over, flinging one arm over his eyes and placing the other one low on his belly. His jaw had grown scruffy, and even in rest, his biceps could have made the cover of any fitness magazine.

Shamelessly drinking in the length of him, she gulped when she noticed the bulge straining against his jeans. If he had been wearing those PJs he had on the other day, she would have had a better view.

She slowly sipped her coffee, but didn't stop ogling. Not like he could see her—he was sound asleep. Staying angry at him was impossible when he looked so cozy and sexy and irresistible. Daydreams taunted her. Oh, how she could release that squished up bulge. She could climb on top of him and allow him to awaken to sweet release. He had granted her a delicious orgasm the other day. She owed him.

"See something you like?"

His husky voice made her jump, causing a good splash of coffee to spill over the top of her mug.

When had he woken up?

He swung his legs to the floor, but didn't stop staring back at her, even as she licked the dripping coffee off the side of her mug.

"I take it you're feeling better this morning." He leaned forward, resting his elbows on his knees. His eyes pierced through her embarrassed fog and lit up her damaged soul.

"I feel great, thanks for asking," she squeaked. She cleared her throat and stood. "I made you breakfast."

"You did?"

"You don't have to sound so surprised."

"I guess I shouldn't be, considering you make your dog's food." He smiled.

She couldn't see it with her back turned to him, but gosh darn it, she could hear it. She could *feel* it.

Savannah handed him the mug-of-muffin, along with a spoon. He raised his brow as he looked back and forth between the muffin and the mug.

"It's a microwaved muffin in a mug." Why was her

voice so weak today?

"Ahh. I was wondering how you managed to bake in here." He poked the chocolate confection with the spoon before digging in. Oops, maybe she should have cut it up into pieces.

Savannah watched him as he took a bite. His expression was one of good humor, but not pleasure. She waited for his feedback while he chewed. And chewed. And chewed.

Okay, she wasn't a baker. She wasn't much of a cook, either. She was a single woman who enjoyed take-out and prepared food that simply required an oven for reheating.

But how bad could it be?

He smiled.

Phew. That was a good sign.

He took another bite.

She released her pent up breath.

"Here, I'll get you some coffee."

"Mmm, thanks," he mumbled around his mouthful of muffin.

She poured the coffee, then whipped around to ask him if he wanted cream or sugar.

He was making the most godawful face! And spitting into a napkin!

"You don't like it?" Savannah nearly dropped the mug *and* the coffee pot. His tongue had been hanging out as if he were airing it. He looked like he wanted to feed the muffin to Rocco.

She slammed the coffee stuff down and stormed over to Quentin, ripping the muffin-in-a-mug out of his hands.

"Hey, I was eating that!"

"You were *making fun* of that."

"No, I was just, uh, you were getting coffee." His voice trailed off. His expression was reminiscent of a young boy caught coloring on the walls.

"I'm sure it's not as bad as you're making it seem."

He sat back on the futon, crossing his arms over his wide chest. Silent. Then a Cheshire cat grin erupted on his face.

"Try it. I dare you."

She huffed and puffed and tossed the mug onto the makeshift counter. "I followed the recipe *exactly*."

"Go ahead and try it. I'm sure you'll love it."

She wrinkled up her face at him. "I'm sure I will!"

She lifted the mug and selected a new spoon, since she hadn't wrestled his out of his grasp. The muffin *smelled* good. How bad could it be?

She took a giant bite. Not bad at all.

Although...

"Ick!" She spit the bite of muffin into a napkin, hurrying to guzzle down her now-lukewarm coffee. "What the hell?"

He didn't just laugh—he guffawed. Rocco ran and put his front paws on Quentin's lap, seemingly trying to figure out what was happening to the man.

"Why didn't you warn me?" She threw a crumpled napkin at him. Rocco quickly retrieved the piece of trash and began ripping it to shreds.

Quentin rose from the futon, striding toward her with a predatory glint in his eye.

"Coming for more?" she taunted, holding the mug out to him.

He didn't answer, but possessively grabbed her hips and pulled them to him. Her body reacted instantly.

"I'm definitely coming for more."

She swallowed, imagining his lower lip being nibbled on. By her. She leaned her head back, preparing for a kiss.

He bypassed her mouth and went straight for her bare neck, nibbling and licking and nuzzling with his scruffy face. She shivered at the eroticism of having him take ownership of her most vulnerable spot.

"You get lonely." Quentin didn't pose a question—he presented his words as fact.

She struggled to string words together.

"No I don't."

He withdrew, making a you-can't-fool-me-because-I'm-smarter-than-I-look face.

"You talk to your dog. And you're nicer to him than you are to any people."

"He likes it," she bristled. "And he accepts me the way I am."

"Guess he and I have that in common." Quentin swooped in and claimed her neck once again. He nibbled a trail over her shoulder (who would have thought that area could be such an erogenous zone?) He pressed his body into hers to keep her upright against the wall as he used a free hand to pull down her neckline the slightest bit, giving him an all-access pass to her sensitive collarbone.

She moaned. Damn him!

"I seem to remember that you always liked my attention in this area." His mouth followed the bone while his hand drifted to her breast.

He remembered correctly. And she couldn't think of one single lover, aside from him, who had ever discovered this about her.

"I remember all of your secret spots." His breath was warm as his words fanned across the trail of moisture he had left. "I fantasize about them all the time."

Her eyes rolled back in her head in an overload of pleasure. Ten years apart hadn't dimmed one fucking thing.

She struggled against him—not really *struggling*, but she felt like she was being strong, trying desperately to regain some semblance of control.

"Aren't we in a fight?" She whispered the words, groaning and writhing at the effects of his persistent mouth and teeth.

His denial vibrated against her throat. She arched her back, driving her hips and breasts into him.

"I seem to remember that we weren't getting along last night. Ohhhh," she whimpered. Her hands went to his chest in a half-hearted attempt to call a cease-fire. "You were angry."

He pulled away and straightened to his full height. She looked up at him, expecting him to step away.

"You're absolutely right. You have some making up to do."

"I made you a muffin," she blurted out.

She didn't think his eyebrows could go any higher without hitting the ceiling.

"Like I said, you owe me."

Savannah dragged her finger in swirls across his chest.

"What do you have in mind?" Even to her own ears, she sounded like a sex-phone operator. He did dangerous things to her libido. He even made her forget why she was so upset with him in the first place.

He leaned in for a kiss, but lingered over her lips. Sparks shot between them—tingly, painful, delicious. Why wasn't he kissing her yet?

Quentin continued to tease—keeping his lips only millimeters away from hers. She tried to close the space, but he wouldn't allow it. He kissed her eyelids, her cheeks, the space below her ear, and a trail across her face to the corner of her mouth. Her body had relaxed to the point that if he removed his hands from her hips, she'd collapse in a heap of mush. She'd give him anything. Do anything. Be anything.

As long as he kissed her the way she needed him to.

"So you agree?" His deep voice vibrated in her ear, creating an erotic warmth that threatened to burn her into ash.

"Mmm." She reached out and captured his earlobe between her teeth.

His turn to sigh.

"Excellent. Joey and I will pick you up at three." He sealed the deal with the kiss she had been longing for, preventing her from voicing her objections.

And then he pulled away and kissed her on the nose.

On the *nose!*

Savannah shouted at him as he practically freaking *danced* to the door.

"That wasn't fair!"

He blew a kiss to her, gave Rocco one more head rubbing, then slammed the door shut behind him, all while Savannah maintained a glare so long she hoped her grandmother wasn't right about faces freezing that way.

Savannah slunk to the floor, back against the wall, burying her head in her hands.

She might as well accept the inevitable—that Quentin and his cherub-faced son would be whisking her away for some sort of mysterious date. She had blown off ice cream night. She had given Quentin a hard time about making her babysit.

She couldn't let the kid down again, and knowing Quentin, he probably already made promises.

Besides, if she had plans with Quentin, she couldn't possibly stop by for dinner with her parents like her dad had hinted.

Savannah still didn't trust herself around Joey, but she wouldn't be in charge of his care. She'd just be a tag-along.

Not like she had any *good* options. For as long as she was stuck in this town, someone was always going to have something they expected from her.

***

Savannah groaned as she reached way up in the closet. After her run, she had decided to busy herself with cleaning and organizing the studio. Might as well do something nice for her parents since they were letting her stay there. The amount of dust in the place had her sneezing enough to keep a wind turbine generating electricity for weeks.

One more closet to organize and she'd be ready to wash the floors.

Savannah readied the trash bag for another load of junk. Her mother would probably kill her for throwing away so much stuff, but seriously, how many empty egg cartons did one person need?

When she couldn't reach the box in the corner of the closet shelf, she dragged a chair over to assist her. After a bit of a struggle to dislodge the thing, she finally succeeded. It was lighter than anticipated (compared to the other boxes full of junk.)

Savannah dropped the box to the floor, sneezing again when a cloud of dust flew into her face.

She settled in beside the box, shooing Rocco away when he tried to nose his way in. If she found a dead animal in here, she'd scream. Or set the studio on fire.

Confusion marbled her thoughts as she dug through the box. What was this? And then she knew. The small, fading scraps of memorabilia—an old ticket stub to a school play, stuck-together Pokemon cards, a clear baggie with brown hair clippings, scribbles drawn by the unsure hand of a young child—all were linked to memories of her sweet brother. Of Brandon.

Not Over You

She held each memory to her heart, and then placed a kiss on every item. She lifted the small blue teddy bear from the box, hugging it as tightly as she wished she could hug her brother.

Savannah smiled at the memory of giving her brother the blue bear. She and Quentin had taken him to the local fair when her parents were too busy to do so. Savannah hadn't been happy about it—a younger brother was a huge inconvenience when she wanted to be alone with her boyfriend and maybe meet up with her friends—but Quentin had insisted it would be fun. Quentin had alternated between carrying Brandon on his shoulders and Savannah on his back for most of the night. He took Brandon on the rides that Savannah didn't want to go on, and allowed Brandon to drag them from game to game, spending Quentin's entire paycheck on useless games. When Quentin kept striking out on winning a prize and Savannah had made fun of him, he offered for her to give it a try. He nearly fell over when she won on the first attempt. Brandon had triumphantly carried that stupid little bear all around for months. And when he became "too old" to carry a stuffed bear, he kept the toy hidden in his bed.

Savannah tucked the bear into her shirt with its fluffy little head sticking out the top. Hands free, she pulled out several more things, including the baseball shirt Brandon had been wearing when he earned his very first trophy.

Emotion clogged her throat. If she deserved to cry, this would be the time. But no, if she had been a better sister, Brandon would be alive today. There wouldn't be a stupid box full of stupid mementos of a beautiful life ended too soon.

Because of a stupid sister.

She whipped the bear out of her shirt and tossed it back in the box, along with the other items. She closed the box up tight, and then returned it to its hiding spot. As she was getting off the chair, another box caught her eye.

Savannah paused before reaching for the new box, considering how much she could handle. She deserved this torture. The building pressure in her temples. The stabbing sensation in the back of her eyes. The storm in her gut.

The fleeting comfort of holding things that represented her brother; precious items he had held and loved. The painful, nauseating truth that he wasn't here any longer and it was all her fault.

She didn't know why she took herself down to the lake last night. She supposed it was her way of slicing open the emotional wound, of bleeding her heart into the place where she had let her brother down. She knew she didn't deserve happiness; that she'd never attain it, anyway.

She knew people thought she was taking her grieving too far. That his death was a tragic accident— one she should move past.

They didn't know her grief. They didn't understand that her brother had been deprived the right to *live*. Being denied the right to move on was the least of the penance she should pay.

The self-inflicted pain nearly crippled her. She

pressed her hand to her heart, then to her stomach. No amount of pressure would save her from bleeding out.

She closed her eyes and took a deep breath. When the cramps eased up, she moved away from the temptation of the closet and turned up the music, watching Rocco drift as far away from the loud tunes as he could.

Isn't this what she did best? Run away from her problems? Tune them out until she didn't have to deal with them anymore?

She started to toss things back into the closet, but knowing there was another box up there made it hard to focus.

Just look in the box. Get it over with.

She didn't have to war with herself for long. If she didn't look at it, she'd be haunted the rest of the time she was here. Might as well rip the bandage off quickly.

She pulled the box down, just as she had the other one.

She gasped as she lifted the flaps and saw things *she* had left behind. Precious mementos of her very own life here in Healing Springs.

Boxed up and stuck in a private closet as if she had died that day, too.

She had always thought her mother was lacking in sentimentality, that she was a bit removed from her children. Yet she kept all of their favorite things, tucked away in enclosed shrines of their lives.

Maybe she wasn't as cold as Savannah had always

imagined. Clearly her mother wasn't so out of touch that she wouldn't know the things to keep. The very items that best represented the lives of her children.

She couldn't keep digging. She hastily packed the few items she had rummaged through, returned the box to its spot, and geared up for another run.

She needed the clean air to chase the dust from her sinuses and her mind.

***

"I didn't know where you planned to go, so I hope this outfit is okay." Savannah gestured to the only non-running t-shirt she had brought. "I didn't exactly bring my whole wardrobe, but I can throw on pants if shorts won't work."

His gaze breezed over her body, and she shivered as goosebumps erupted at his attention. "Perfect."

"I can't leave Rocco for long, so if we can't bring him, I'll have to be back within a couple of hours." Yeah, he'd be fine for longer, but if using Rocco as an excuse could get her out of this date, she'd use it. She had no qualms.

"He is more than welcome. I know you're a package deal." Quentin smiled and winked, and Savannah had the feeling he knew what she was trying to pull. "Come on, boy. You can sit in the back with Joey."

With no backup excuses, Savannah shuffled out to the truck. She greeted Joey with enthusiasm that felt surprisingly genuine. His bright, infectious "kid-ness" warmed her deeply. She never, ever allowed herself to get close—physically or emotionally—to children, but being around this boy reminded her of how much she once loved kids. How she had dreamed of having two of her own. How she had even thought—erroneously—that one day she'd adopt and give a few abused kids a permanent home full of love.

Rocco's face-licking and Joey's belly-giggling pulled her back to the present.

She made a silent promise to herself that for this one afternoon, she wouldn't punish herself. For this one collection of moments, she'd pretend she wasn't a murderer.

"Turn it *up!*" Joey kicked the back of his father's seat as he shouted out his demands.

"If you say so." Quentin winked again at Savannah and turned up the radio. A peppy kid's song filled the cab of the truck, and Savannah found herself dancing along in her seat.

How hard could it be to live in the present for a change? The past would be there for her when she was ready to sleep tonight.

Savannah had been so busy watching Joey sing to Rocco that she didn't notice where they had gone. When she heard the crunching of the truck tires on the sandy parking lot, she looked ahead. She didn't recognize this place, but she knew they had left town.

"Yay! Can we swim?"

Savannah's gut tightened at Joey's request.

"I don't know if the water's warm enough to swim

yet, buddy, but we can definitely go in to your knees."

Savannah took in the sight of the trees and the trail. Did he bring her to a lake? They had driven too far for it to be *the lake*, but she wasn't ready to deal with any body of water (aside from the ocean) without a bottle of liquid strength—the kind she could only get at the liquor store.

Quentin opened her door as she gripped the seat.

"Come on. It'll be fun." Quentin's eyes twinkled. He had no idea what he asked of her.

"Let's go, let's go, *let's go!*" Joey chanted in the back seat, and Rocco eagerly awaited his turn to run wild.

She couldn't ruin this for them.

Reluctantly, she swung her legs out of the truck, hopping down as Rocco jumped out. Quentin climbed in to release Joey from his buckles.

Joey ran ahead down the path. Savannah quickened her pace, not wanting to let him get too far ahead. Quentin grabbed her hand and squeezed.

"It's okay. He knows the way."

She couldn't lie to herself—his hand cradling hers felt nice. Warm. Strong. Protective. Secure.

She hadn't been this intimate with a man since, well, him. All those years ago.

Sex? Yeah, she could maintain her distance even in the midst of the action. Hand-holding and affection? Way more than she allowed.

She didn't pull away. Quentin didn't release her.

A short, anxiety-ridden walk through the woods brought them to a potential crime scene—a body of water eager to swallow up some poor soul. The gently lapping waves washed over rocks and sent chills down her back. Not the good kind of chills. There was a time when the soft sound of the waves and the rippled blue of the water would have soothed her. Now, however, her whole body tightened.

Quentin must have noticed, because he removed his hand from hers and put his arm around her shoulder, pulling her closer to him. He kissed the top of her head.

"Daddy! Look what I found!"

Joey held out a small, flat rock—perfect for skipping.

Quentin gave Savannah a squeeze before releasing her and jogging over to his son. He bent to examine the treasure, and then, showing no sign of understanding the dangers, led his son to the water.

Savannah's heart threatened to thump its way out of her chest. She wanted to look away, but if she let her guard down, something terrible would happen. She stepped closer to the shore, dragging her feet through the sand. Rocco ran wildly along the beach, kicking up a sand storm. To her relief, he stayed away from the water.

Joey kicked off his sneakers. Savannah's heart nearly exploded. She stepped closer, freezing as the boy entered the water. He didn't go past his ankles before he bent down and started digging in the sand with a stick.

Eyes glued to the boy, Savannah didn't notice Quentin throwing a stick for Rocco until it was too late.

Rocco promptly bolted for the water, jumping into the glass-like surface without waiting for permission.

Joey's laughter pierced through the screams in Savannah's head as Rocco splashed the boy. Quentin and Joey began to splash back at the dog, who collected his stick and brought it to the shore to chew on.

Savannah swallowed past the prickly, spiky lump of fear lodged in her desert-dry throat. Body stiff, she stormed over to Quentin.

"Don't do that again." She kept her voice low so as not to frighten Joey, but she wouldn't tolerate Quentin's lack of concern for her dog's safety.

"Do what?" He had the nerve to fake confusion.

"You know what you did. With the stick."

"He loved it. He didn't bring it back to me, but he did fetch it."

Savannah rolled her eyes and moved toward her dog as Joey begged for Quentin's attention.

Seconds later, Quentin was joining her.

"Get back there—your son is still in the water!"

"He's ankle deep. Besides, he's very careful and an excellent swimmer."

"So was Brandon," Savannah shot back. "Brandon was careful and a great swimmer, and he still drowned."

The words sounded like they were delivered to her ears from somewhere far away. From an omnipotent narrator. Someone who could tell the story, but couldn't truly understand the meaning behind the words.

Brandon was careful.
Brandon was a great swimmer.
Brandon drowned.
Brandon was dead.
Brandon was dead.
Brandon was dead.
Shaking, Savannah wrapped her arms around her waist.
Savannah lived.
The wrong Grace child died.
Quentin bent and picked up another stick. He threw it to the water before she could stop him. Rocco chased it, diving in to retrieve the wood.

She struggled to deliver sounds from her vocal cords. When they finally emerged past her tightened throat, the words were no more than a squeak. "What are you doing?"

"He likes the water. It's good for him."

She shook her head, forcing the spots to dance around in front of her eyes. "He could drown. We run, we don't swim."

"He's not going to drown, Peaches. Dogs are built for swimming. Come on, dig with Joey and me."

Savannah couldn't move if she wanted to. Rocco had decided he didn't want to play it safe on the shore any longer. He ran into the water all the way up to his shoulders. He didn't look back. Her throat clamped—she couldn't call him. Couldn't even whistle. Her hands froze in place. She couldn't clap to get his attention.

She could only watch as his head bobbed in the water. Was he flailing? Did he need rescuing?

Or would he simply stop moving eventually? Would they have to drag him out of the water and pronounce him dead?

"Peaches, what's wrong?"

She couldn't respond. Was this what a catatonic state was like?

"Savvy. Savannah!" Quentin grabbed her by the shoulders and shook. "Peaches, everyone is safe."

She snapped back to the present moment in time to watch Rocco swim back to shore. Joey left the water, too, chasing after Rocco along the beach. Her body relaxed as they distanced themselves from the water.

"See? Everyone is fine. They love the water, Savannah."

Was he really so dense? Didn't he see the danger? How could he allow his son to play in a place that could turn deadly in an instant?

"You've got to hear me, Peaches. What happened to Brandon was an accident. A horrible, tragic accident."

Savannah lifted her hands to her ears, backing away. Quentin grabbed her elbows, stilling her. She glared at him.

"It was a terrible accident. It won't happen again. Joey is safe. Rocco is safe. You are safe."

"Wasn't once enough?" She hoped her eyes cut him as deeply as his words cut her. She was powerless, helpless. She only had anger to fight this battle for her.

Anger and her legs. Legs that could carry her away.

She turned away from Quentin, tapping her thigh

to call Rocco to her.

"Where are you going?" Quentin demanded.

"I'm leaving."

"Don't be crazy. We're three towns away."

"I have perfectly good feet to carry me."

"Savannah, don't." Quentin intercepted her, blocking her way. "Let's work through this. Together."

"There's nothing to work through, Quentin. My brother is dead. He *died*. He died while I was busy making out with *you*. I wasn't paying attention to him and now he's gone. I'm not going to ever make that mistake again."

She stalked toward the parking lot, halting only when she heard Joey crying.

Dammit. She hadn't even thought of how her abrupt departure might affect him.

She turned around in time to see his little legs pumping hard to catch up.

"Where are you going?" Joey asked, his eyes filled with trepidation.

"I have to go, sweetie. I didn't mention this before, but I don't really like the beach." His eyes widened and became as watery as the puddles that formed in the holes close to the shoreline. "I'm sorry."

"You'll like it better if you come in the water. I'll help you." Joey grabbed her hand and tried to drag her forward.

Quentin stepped in.

"Actually, buddy, it's time to go. I thought maybe we could have ice cream for dinner on the way home."

Savannah considered that she may have come

down with an instant case of Stockholm syndrome, because she suddenly felt gratitude toward her captor. That short-lived gratitude at his intervention didn't stop her from shooting daggers at him as she lifted herself into the truck. Luckily, the forbidden promise of ice cream for dinner prevented a fit at their abrupt departure from the lake.

The entire ride, Savannah beat herself up internally.

She wasn't normal. She wasn't okay.

She'd never be okay.

"Daddy, I did good. I didn't cry."

"That's right, buddy. You listened very nicely when it was time to go."

"Savannah almost cried, though. She didn't like the water. Girls don't like sand and water and dirt and stuff, right, Daddy?"

Quentin laughed at his son's logic. Savannah stiffened. She most certainly did not almost cry!

"Girls are mysterious creatures, son." Quentin reached over and gently squeezed Savannah's thigh.

"Don't be silly, Joey. I don't cry."

"You don't?" Joey's little cupid mouth dropped to his chest. "Girls always cry. Boys cry too, right, Daddy? 'Cept we're not 'sposed to cry when we have to leave places or daddies won't bring us back. Right, Daddy?"

"That's right. It's good to cry sometimes." Quentin looked to Savannah. She had the eerie suspicion that he could see right through her.

"Daddy cries sometimes, too. Like when we watch movies."

Not Over You

"Hey now. No giving away my secrets."

Joey laughed. Savannah smiled. She remembered his propensity for sniffling during sad parts and pretending his eyes were irritated.

"When do you cry?" Joey seemed to be asking Savannah, but she tried to ignore the question.

He was relentless.

"I told you. I don't cry."

"Everybody cries!" Joey argued. "Does Rocco cry?"

"Rocco cries all the time. Especially when it takes me too long to get his food ready."

Joey fell into a fit of laughter, forcing a smile to erupt through the cracks of Savannah's stone face and resolve. Seemingly mid-laugh, he slumped over in his car seat and fell asleep.

"Is he okay?" Savannah turned to check for breathing.

Quentin laughed. "Oh, yeah. He can't usually make it through a car ride without a nap. He's always so go, go, go, but when he finally gets tired, he zonks right out."

Savannah breathed in relief, then turned back to watch the road.

"When's the last time you cried, Peaches?"

Quentin's voice took on a serious note now that his son was unconscious. She knew he was probing, but she couldn't resist the comfort he offered.

"Ten years ago."

"Ten years? You haven't cried in ten years?"

She shook her head, but stared out the side window at the blur of trees and shrubs.

"Have you been to his stone?"

Six words. Sharper than twenty-six knives wielded at her heart. Why must everyone ask her? Didn't they know how the thought of seeing her brother in that cold, hard place made her want to crawl out of her skin?

"Have you been there yet, Savannah?"

She tried to answer, but her throat closed once again.

"Can I take you there?"

"No." Squeaky, but firm.

"I think it could help you."

"You know what could help me? Getting me home."

She sat up straight in her seat, pulling at the seatbelt as it cut into her neck. The sooner she returned to the studio, the sooner she could put this terrible day behind her.

The rest of the ride was silent, aside from the kid music that still hummed quietly under the roar of the engine.

Joey lifted his head when Savannah opened the truck door and the breeze hit his face. He reached out to touch Rocco one last time and mumbled something to Savannah. Savannah threw the boy a kiss and thanked him for a wonderful date, even though the day was anything but wonderful. Still, it wasn't the child's fault she was screwed up. Heck, it wasn't even Quentin's fault.

This dysfunction was all on her.

And the realization served as further proof of what

Not Over You

she already knew.
She could never have a future with Quentin.

Chapter Ten

Savannah blamed Rocco for her temporary insanity. He was the one who looked at her with the cocked-head concern. He was the one who pushed her out of bed with his giant snout. He was the one who paced around miserably and then refused to eat his food.

Her sadness was affecting not only her own life, but her dog's happiness, too.

So the fact that she was now strolling down Main Street on a Sunday morning, faking a smile, was *all his fault*.

Since arriving to town, she had been ruled by her emotions. Her pain had been allowed to fester, to gush, to throb.

She'd never get over the death of her brother. She'd never stop punishing herself for what happened. But she didn't have to keep her poor dog locked away from civilization in order to wallow in her own self pity. Back home, Rocco was practically the town mascot. He didn't appreciate being isolated here.

Not Over You

Rocco wagged his tail stump as he sniffed every tree, every corner, every lamppost. Eager for sensory input, he practically smiled when another dog allowed him to sniff its butt.

So far, Savannah hadn't recognized anyone. She hoped to keep it that way, but since she had chosen to project a sunnier disposition for the day, she was prepared to act more like a decent human being and not the raging anti-social she wished she could be.

"Stop right there, young lady. Don't you dare walk by Miss Molly without a hello!"

Savannah stopped short, taking a deep breath before turning toward the old woman. Miss Molly, one of the town's matriarchs, sat in a wrought iron chair outside of her gift shop. The eccentric old woman had skin as smooth as a baby's bottom, leading visitors to believe she bathed in the springs and was healed. Her shoulders slouched, and she had a giant hump on her back, giving away her age. She had lost an eye in a freak accident many years ago, but she used that as an opportunity to accessorize. Her eye patches were legendary—a different style every day. Today she donned a blue fleece fabric with white daisies.

"Get over here, young lady." Miss Molly held her arms open. Savannah smiled as she leaned over to embrace the elderly woman. She smelled of rosewater and lavender, just like always.

Savannah made small talk and introduced the smiley woman to Rocco. Rocco ate up the attention Miss Molly bestowed upon him.

"Pull up that seat over there and tell me what kind

of life you've made for yourself. Speak up so I can hear you."

Savannah shared as much as she comfortably could about her life in the seaside town in Maine. She glossed over the ugly details.

When Savannah ran out of surface things to share, Miss Molly's stare intensified.

"You were our golden girl, Savvy darling. Everyone had high expectations for the things you would accomplish in this world." Miss Molly reached across the rickety table and placed her hands over Savannah's. "Folks here in Healing Springs may have had their own ideas of what you'd become, but I think you've done a damn good job of making a life for yourself."

Savannah studied Miss Molly's hands—after generations of giving love and guidance to residents of all ages, they were now filled with road maps and trails long ago traveled.

"I'm just glad I lived long enough to see you come home."

"Miss Molly, town legend has it that you bathe in the fountain of youth and will live forever." Savannah's smile felt genuine for a change. Being around someone as sweet and positive as Miss Molly had that effect on people.

Miss Molly laughed. "You're as much a charmer as that boy of yours."

"I don't have a boy, other than Rocco."

Rocco's ears turned back at the sound of his name. He looked at Savannah, then made a low grumble and sat on Miss Molly's feet. When Savannah tried to call him off, Miss Molly waved her hand in the air and said he was perfectly welcome to warm her toes.

"You may be able to fool yourself, young lady, but Miss Molly sees everything."

Savannah felt the hairs rise on her arms.

"I've heard rumblings that you're only here for a short while, but I think you and I both know that you can't deny the pull you have to this town. To these people. To one boy in particular."

Savannah's foot began to tap under the table. A run would be so good right now. Her muscles ached for the burn.

She tried to pull away, but Miss Molly tightened her hold.

"I know you have the urge to get away. To hide from your feelings. You have the same look in those lovely eyes as you did the last day I saw you way back in the dark time. For the past ten years, I have regretted not helping you on the last day I saw you. Savvy, let me help you."

"It wasn't your job to help me. I didn't deserve it then, and I don't deserve it now." Savannah straightened her spine and crossed one leg over the other, bumping her foot into the center leg of the table. She clenched her teeth, tightening her jaw. She respected Miss Molly a great deal, more than she did most people, so she bit back the words she normally used to keep people at a distance.

"Savvy darling, you've got to learn to forgive yourself. I can see your soul, young lady. I may only have this one good eye, but I could see your sadness even if I were blind. You must stop blaming yourself for things you couldn't control."

Savannah opened her mouth to object, but Miss Molly held her hand up to quiet her.

"You were a child. What happened to your brother could have happened under anyone's care. Look me in my eye."

Savannah did as told. She had looked up to Miss Molly throughout her entire childhood and teen years. When Savannah was a knobby-kneed eight-year-old, Miss Molly had given her free candy every time she wandered into the store. When she was twelve, Miss Molly gave her her first job dusting the shelves in the gift shop. When she was sixteen, Miss Molly taught her how to fill out college applications and regaled her with stories of powerful women in history.

Miss Molly had provided a listening ear when Savannah's best friend had hurt her feelings when she was ten. She helped her hang posters around town when the stray cat she adopted went missing when Savannah was thirteen. She intervened when a pack of mean boys chased her through town with a snake in their hands when Savannah was seven.

She couldn't be rude to Miss Molly.

"You've got to forgive yourself." Miss Molly leaned forward, moaning a little at the effort. "And you've got to forgive your mother."

"Wh—"

"Hush, girl. Don't deny what I can plainly see. I've heard the rumors, and I'm sure some of them have a grain of truth. I know you're here to save your mother. But what she needs more than your blood is your love. She lost her only two children that day. It's hard for a mom to get past that."

A lead ball settled into Savannah's gut, weighing her down and preventing her from storming off the way she would have if anyone else had uttered these words to her. Rocco sat happily beside the elderly woman, his head resting on her lap. Miss Molly had a healing effect on everyone she came in contact with.

"Now before you go, place all your worries into the worry jar. Go on, you know the drill."

"Miss Molly, you know I respect you more than anyone in the world, but I don't think the worry jar is going to help me."

"Nonsense. Write your worries on the paper, crumple it up good, and drop it in the jar. I'll be releasing them to the universe in a couple of days. Go on, now." Miss Molly sat back in her chair and crossed her arms over her belly. She winked at Savannah as Savannah hesitated to commit to doing as told. "It's confidential."

"Miss Molly..."

"No more out of you. Get on in there and ask Riley if you need some help. Remember Riley? My little great-granddaughter? She's all grown up now and working the shop on weekends, just like you used to do."

Savannah smiled. She did remember Riley. Riley was in Brandon's grade. They had the kind of love/hate relationship that only eight-year-olds could perfect.

"I'll sit here and watch your dog for you. I assure you that my releasing of the worry jar contents is completely environmentally friendly, and no one ever reads the sacred words written on the paper. Top secret."

Savannah bent over to hug Miss Molly before complying with Miss Molly's wishes. Really, what could it hurt? She'd scribble a few words onto the paper if it helped Miss Molly feel better.

Riley didn't seem to remember Savannah, and Savannah didn't bother to refresh her memory, but she did enjoy a brief conversation about the new shop décor. Savannah was surprised to find that her mood had lightened considerably since she left the studio this morning.

By the time she said her goodbyes to her old friend and mentor, Savannah's shoulders were more relaxed and her step was less tense.

Rocco must have noticed the change in her, because he became more playful than he had been since pulling into town. She stopped on the common for some rough-and-tumble play, stopping to reassure the stroller-pushing group of moms that though he looked big and vicious, the only danger he posed to children was the possibility of knocking them off unsteady feet while licking their faces.

While Rocco explored the base of a tree trunk, Savannah's phone started buzzing with an incoming call. She hit "ignore" when she saw it was Quentin. Why would he be calling? She sort of figured she'd never hear from him again after yesterday's disaster.

Not Over You

The mention of Quentin's name by a group of women had Savannah tuning in to their conversation, all while ignoring the fact that her phone was buzzing again. They gestured wildly toward the giant canvas-covered monstrosity on the other side of the common, near the pond. Their voices got hush-hush, and then they turned toward her. Ashamed at being caught eavesdropping, Savannah called Rocco and continued down the main path and out to the other side of the common, where her car was parked.

"What now, Rocco?"

Rocco cocked his head as if weighing his options. She filled his travel bowl with fresh water and waited for him to finish lapping it up.

She sat in the driver's seat without turning the key.

"Really, Rocco? You think we should?" Rocco groaned in response. "I don't know. I'm not sure we should just stop by Mom and Dad's house."

After visiting with Miss Molly, Savannah had been left with the realization that though she'd never be whole again, there was a giant part of her heart that could heal. She had to admit to herself that her whole reason for coming here was to try to bring her mother back to good health. If Miss Molly was right—and considering the boxes Savannah had found in Mom's studio, she had to be—Mom needed emotional healing as well.

Savannah had never considered the fact that her mother would have had to mourn the loss of her daughter, too. She had always figured her mother would have been happy to be rid of her. To not have a daily reminder of her son's tragic death. To not have to look at the face of the person who should have been more careful.

Savannah had found nothing but acceptance since she came back to town. She had half-expected to be chased out with pitchforks. Her mother hadn't been warm and friendly, but could Savannah blame her? She had to be honest—Savannah hadn't exactly been the picture of sunshine and joy herself.

The blood test results would be in tomorrow. Savannah would be heading back to her life, away from this place. She'd come back when it was time for the donation (if she couldn't politely persuade her stepdad to allow her to donate from a distance), but her time here would be put behind her.

Before she left, she knew she had to do her best to make amends with her mother. To let her know that leaving ten years ago was Savannah's own doing. To apologize for killing her only son. To beg forgiveness for not being there for the funeral.

And maybe—just maybe…

Savannah shook her head at the crazy thoughts flooding her head.

Maybe she could fix things enough to stay.

Maybe there was the tiniest of possibilities that she could have the life she had always dreamed about. With Quentin.

Savannah's lap buzzed with an incoming text. Huh, her stepdad. They must have been on the same wavelength.

Savannah opened the text and clenched her teeth so tight that she bit her tongue in the process.

"Meet me at the hospital. Your mother was brought by ambulance."

Immediately after reading that horrifying text, another popped up, this time from Quentin.

"Your mom is okay, but you might want to come see her. She's being admitted to ICU. I can pick you up and fill you in if you want."

Chapter Eleven

Savannah wiped her sweating palms on her shorts as she paused outside her mother's room. She had parked in the shade and left the windows open for Rocco, but she knew she couldn't leave him there long. She had no idea what medically had happened, but she didn't think it was a coincidence that her mood had lifted just before her mother fell ill.

This was why Savannah needed to constantly punish herself.

Bad things happened because of her.

The bright fluorescent lights combined with her shallow breathing threatened to knock Savannah out cold. She leaned against the cheerfully painted yellow wall for support. Her stepfather was suddenly in front of her, his hands on her shoulders, concern in his eyes. She must have managed to convince him that she was fine, because as his face grew bigger and smaller and closer and farther, he kept talking. What was he saying? Oh, complications. Something about chemotherapy. Something else about expediting the donation process. He used big words that she couldn't wrap her mind around. She felt like she was floating in front of him. She had no awareness of her feet—did she leave them somewhere?

Dad led her to her mother's bedside. Mom was connected to all sorts of beeping, humming machines. Sound asleep. A dried trail of tears on the side of her mother's face cut directly into Savannah's heart, making her wish she were the one in the bed instead.

Savannah kissed her mother's head, still not feeling like she had any control over her body.

"I'll give you a minute alone," Dad said before leaving the room.

Savannah wanted to scream out to him—to beg him not to leave. Savannah couldn't be trusted. But her throat was too tight and her mind too foggy to say a thing.

Words wouldn't come, so Savannah sat in the chair by the bed and watched her mother's chest rise and fall with each breath. She looked frail. Old. Beaten by life.

Not at all like the strong, stoic mother who had raised Savannah.

Savannah noticed her own throat vibrating before she realized she had begun to softly hum. A silent tear leaked from her mother's eye, running down to the sterile-white pillow and quickly absorbing into the cotton.

She was humming the same tune her mother used to hum while rocking Brandon. She couldn't remember, but she thought her mother may have hummed it to Savannah when she was younger, too.

Savannah's mother reached a hand out without opening her eyes. In a trance, Savannah met her partway. They linked their fingers together as Savannah continued to hum. She leaned forward and kissed her mother's smooth knuckles.

Her mom tightened her grip. Almost immediately, the machines began to beep like crazy and a team of nurses came rushing into the room. Savannah was pushed to the side, and without waiting to see what happened, she ran.

***

Stumbling down the paved trail, Savannah tried to talk herself into going to the bar instead. This was a terrible, horrible, worst-ever idea.

She didn't know the exact location of her destination, but she had a hunch.

Savannah hadn't managed to shake the trance she had been in at the hospital. She felt like she was watching herself. Watching as she parked the car near the metal gate, leaving the keys in the ignition, the door wide open, and the reminder alarm dinging. Watching as she marched down the rolling hill toward the sunset. Watching as Rocco stayed close to her side. Watching as she passed old landmarks which told her she was heading to the right area.

Watching as she found Brandon's headstone.

Watching as she fell to the ground.

And then she could watch no more.

Hot pain shot through her gut, like someone had stabbed her with a searing fireplace poker. Vomit gathered in her throat. Her breaths came fast and shallow, forcing her shoulders up and down and her head to become even lighter.

Trembling, she reached out and traced the letters on the stone. Her fingers recoiled at the coldness of the rock. Her ears rang with her tortured gasp.

Brandon would be so cold in there. In the ground.

Savannah wrapped her arms around the headstone, desperate to share her warmth. Maybe if she warmed the stone enough, the warmth would penetrate down. She pressed her cheek against the carved picture of her brother in his baseball uniform. In life, he had been full of vigor and joy. Etched into an eternal memory on this headstone, he looked like he could jump off and beg her to pitch the ball at any moment.

"I'm sorry, Brandon. I'm so, so sorry."

She clutched the stone tighter, ignoring the thorny bushes digging into her thighs. She didn't care that the rough edge of the stone cut into her palms—she tightened her grip anyway.

The first sob surprised her as it shot out of her with the force of a caged-for-too-long lioness. As tears gushed out of her eyes and trailed into her open mouth, she sobbed harder. No dam in the world could hold in this anguish—no amount of self-flagellation could stop this tsunami of emotion.

Rocco nudged at her arms, trying to get between her and what he must have assumed was the source of this uncharacteristic outburst. She could offer him no comfort—she was too lost. Too gone. She turned her head away so he wouldn't see her tears and continued to release the emotion that had been turned off for so many years.

Her shoulders ached from clenching the stone, and her screams echoed off the surrounding trees and back to her, kicking her in the throat.

But she couldn't let go.

She couldn't leave Brandon alone. Not again.

She should be in that ground.

Strong hands gripped her arms, carefully prying her away from the stone, pulling her to her feet, and turning her into a warm chest. She didn't have the strength to pull away. She didn't have the strength to hide her tears. The only thing she could do was clench his stiff uniform shirt and continue to bleed out her emotions.

***

Quentin held her as tight as he could—partly so she wouldn't fall, partly because he wanted to squeeze out this demon she'd been carrying around for a decade.

He whispered words meant to soothe as she sobbed harder and harder, soaking his shirt and piercing his heart.

This was good. He had to believe it. She had come to the cemetery on her own. She had come face to face with her brother's stone. She had to process the emotions in order to heal. He closed his eyes and prayed that he was right. He had listened to a whole lot of psycho-babble over the years, and never had anyone ever said it was better to keep emotions bottled inside.

She was releasing her sadness.

This had to be good.

At the moment, it felt like torture. Her quiet sadness and pain had been difficult. This was like being kicked in the nuts over and over.

None of his paramedic training had prepared him for this.

He had gone up to her mother's hospital room, hoping to run into her. When Rick told him that Karyn had crashed and Savannah had disappeared, Quentin's blood had turned to ice in his veins. Savannah was in too fragile of a state. Every terrible scenario he could imagine ran through his head as he had sprinted to his truck. He'd find her. He'd help her. He wouldn't let anything bad happen to her again.

He didn't know how he knew to come here. But as she clawed at his chest and poured out her anguish, he was so glad he did. She shouldn't be alone at a time like this. She shouldn't have been alone ten years ago. He never should have left her side, no matter how much she had pushed him away. He never should have given her the opportunity to leave town.

Quentin kissed the top of her head. She began to sink lower. He tightened his grip. He'd hold her up forever—she didn't deserve to be in the mud.

"It's all my fault." Savannah's muffled cries tore

him to pieces with their jagged, broken edges. Hot tears gathered in his eyes as he relived the exact feelings he had experienced way back then.

"No. It was never your fault."

"I should be in the ground, not him. I *deserve* to be in the ground." She hiccupped and wailed, hitting his chest with feeble punches. He grabbed her wrists, stilling the motion.

"Savannah. No." He kissed her knuckles. "Trading one life for another is not what anyone would ever want. Brandon certainly wouldn't want that."

"Brandon would want to be alive! He would want to run across the grass, not be buried beneath it!" Her anger dissolved as quickly as it came, driving more tears to the surface and making her gasp for air.

Quentin lowered them to the ground, pulling her onto his lap and cradling her against his chest.

"He never thrashed in the water. If I had known he was in trouble, I would have helped him. I didn't know."

"I know, baby. No one knew."

"I didn't know that drowning could be so, so," she hiccupped. "So silent."

"I didn't either. Not until then."

"Why didn't anyone ever tell us? I thought I'd hear something. I thought there'd be a warning."

He stroked her arm and showered kisses upon her head. He didn't know how to help her. How to heal her.

All he knew was how to love her.

"I don't know how to live without him. I can go

through the motions of living, but I'm no more alive than the picture on his stone."

Quentin led her hand to his chest, placing it on his beating heart.

"Feel that?"

Savannah's swollen, red-rimmed eyes stared at their joined hands. She nodded slowly.

"I'm alive." He placed their joined hands over her heart. "You're alive." He cupped her chin and raised it toward him. "Our love is alive."

He kissed her gently, not wanting to distract her from her mourning—only wanting to reassure her that he was here for her.

"I don't know how to be happy."

He wasn't sure he heard her right. Her words were small, quiet, faint. But they replayed over and over in his head until he was certain.

"Let me help you."

She relaxed into his embrace and fell fast asleep.

Chapter Twelve

Savannah awoke to a raging headache and a crook in her neck. Apparently all that crap she had heard about crying being a cleansing release was BS. She didn't feel better—she felt like a gang of giants had danced across her forehead and eyeballs.

She didn't mind the crook in the neck, though, since it was simply a side effect of sleeping in her hero's arms.

She smiled up at his scruffy chin, pushing herself onto her elbow so she could get a good look at him sleeping.

Yesterday had probably been the worst day in recent history, but today was off to a great start.

Once Quentin had assured her that her mother was okay, she had been able to relax a bit. Seeing Brandon's stone and finally allowing herself to grieve had helped in some small way—though she wasn't sure she'd admit it to anyone.

Maybe Miss Molly's worry jar thing had some sort of magical property after all.

Quentin woke up under her perusal, catching her

staring. He smiled and mussed her hair, then pulled her in for a bear hug. Nose pressed against his chest, she fought for a breath. How did he manage to smell so delicious? Even pre-shower. If she were to die of smothering, this was definitely the way she'd want to go.

His hands began to massage her back, finding the pain in her neck immediately. She moaned into his touch, amazed at his ability to sense pain and heal it.

She thought she'd be more embarrassed to have had him see her cry. But he never made her feel bad about herself.

"Hey, Quentin."

His slow, seductive smile awakened her in a completely different way. Her body pressed closer to his. His hand moved down to the curve of her ass, stroking, swirling, teasing.

"Yes, my Peaches?"

"Thank you."

He rolled over so she was pinned beneath him, his body—his eager, ready body if the poking in her hip was any indication—pressed to hers.

"You have absolutely nothing to thank me for. I'm the one who is thankful here."

She put her hands on the sides of his face. Was there any man more perfect?

She knew the answer. She had met plenty of men. None were as selfless, giving, loving, accepting. Never mind the fact that he was built like a male stripper. His lean, muscular physique certainly didn't cost him any points in the "you-can-be-every-month-in-the-hot-guy-calendar" department.

Her hands drifted into his hair. She loved the way he closed his eyes when she stroked his head. She tugged his ears to bring his lips to hers. He didn't put up a fight.

His kiss had the power to make the world spin. Though scientist might disagree, she knew for a fact that what he did to her was the single reason the planet continued orbiting the sun.

His tongue played with hers, swooping, stroking, waltzing. He nipped her bottom lip playfully, and she punished him with a hair tug and a deeper kiss.

He moaned, clearly approving of her punishment.

He adjusted himself so his hand could roam down her body—meandering over her curves and finding a resting spot on her hip. He massaged deeply as his tongue continued to wreak havoc with hers.

His fingers danced lower, to the top of her panties. He must have removed her pants before they went to sleep last night. She sighed. She moaned. With her hips thrusting upward, she invited him to enter without knocking.

He continued teasing, letting his fingers skim her lower abdomen. His kisses trailed off to her ear, then her neck, all while his fingertips grazed the top of her private hairline. She shivered at the delicate intrusion, wanting him to plunge lower.

Quentin's tongue danced over her collarbone while his hands pushed her shirt up, revealing her bra. His hot breath shot through the thin fabric, pebbling her nipples immediately. She arched and moaned, which made him laugh and tease even more.

What was she telling herself about him being the perfect man? Because as soon as she became capable of forming a coherent thought, she was so changing her mind!

The man tortured. And he *delighted* in his torture! The nerve!

His laughter came to an abrupt halt when she managed to get her hands down the front of his pants.

"Not so funny now, huh?"

Quentin grunted and groaned and thrust himself into her hand. She squeezed as he lost himself to the feelings she had been dying to give him.

His erection pulsed in her hand. Silky and strong. She slid her hand down his length, moaning when moisture from his tip slickened her hand. She wanted all of him. In her. On her. With her.

She craved his touch. Became desperate to taste him. Needed him to fill her.

He pulled her hand away without any warning, then pinned both of her arms up over her head. He kissed her arm, nuzzled her neck.

She was going to die from the flame he lit in her. Dammit, he should have been a firefighter so he could put her fire out with his hose.

"Give me your hose."

Oops.

He stopped mid-nuzzle and studied her face with the most quizzical and comical of looks. Why did she say that? How did he manage to break her filter?

"I'm sure you think you heard me say something

really crazy, but I assure you it was not me."

"Really, now? So it wasn't you who was asking for my hose? 'Cause I gotta tell ya, that's not a request I hear often."

She cursed herself for blushing. Blushing! Like a thirteen-year-old being given her first kiss.

Savannah didn't blush—not at times like these. She was a master seductress. Or something like that.

"Just get down here and kiss me."

"*That* I can do."

Before his lips fulfilled her demand, his phone vibrated on the nightstand.

Immediately after it began vibrating, a young voice started calling out, "Daddy, pick up! Daddy, pick up!" Over and over until Quentin rolled away from her to silence the phone.

"Why did I think it was a great idea to set his voice as my ringtone?"

Savannah laughed. That was worse than the time her mother walked in on them in this very studio when she was sixteen.

"You'd better call him back before he comes looking for you."

While Quentin returned his son's call, she went to the bathroom to splash cool water on her face.

She smiled around her toothbrush as she listened to his caring, fatherly tone. He made her knees weak in so many ways.

Moments later, when he pulled her in for a hip-to-hip hug and a smoldering kiss goodbye, she informed him that she'd be hanging with them later today. His face lit up like the neon signs in Atlantic City.

"Assuming you don't mind if I crash your Sunday party?"

"Joey will be thrilled."

"And you?"

He pushed her back against the wall, letting her feel just how thrilled he was.

"Need I say more?"

She reached down to cup him, but he pulled her hand away.

"Later."

And with that promise, he left her in the studio, all thoughts on just what she would do with him when she finally had him at her mercy.

***

"Stay, stay, stay, stay!"

Joey squeezed Savannah's hands and jumped up and down in front of her, begging her for the millionth time to have a slumber party.

His eyes filled with tears and his lower lip jutted out when she said she couldn't.

She looked to Quentin for assistance. He leaned against the doorframe, crossed his arms, and casually inquired as to why she couldn't stay.

Some help he was!

"You know why I can't stay."

"Why? Why? Why? Why?" More jumping. How he managed to have so much energy after the day they spent at the park playing kickball and chasing Rocco was beyond her.

"Yeah, why?" The sparkle in Quentin's eyes made her smile in spite of the intense need she had to throttle him.

She made a sound of disappointment, looked to the ceiling as if she just remembered something important, and said, "Because I don't have my jammies."

"You can sleep in your clothes. Sometimes Daddy lets me if I'm really tired."

"That wouldn't be very comfy, though."

"You can borrow Daddy's. Or Nana Robby's." Such a problem solver, that kid. "You have to stay. Rocco wants to."

Savannah couldn't argue, considering Rocco was sound asleep on the cushions Joey had tossed from the couch to the floor. When she tried to make him move, Quentin and Joey both insisted that he not be disturbed.

"Please? I was so good when you went to see your mommy at the hop-sital." Savannah smiled at his mispronunciation of the word. It was true—when she stopped in to visit her mom, he and Quentin had waited outside with Rocco until her mom had fallen back to sleep.

She breathed deep.

Quentin finally took pity on Savannah and pried Joey off of her hands.

"You go ahead and get your sleeping bag and pillows and stuffies, and I'll keep working on our guest."

She shot him a look that should have left no secret of her intentions. She'd slay him if they were alone.

With Joey whooping in the other room, Savannah tried to look everywhere *but* Quentin's way-too-easy-to-fall-for face. Guess how long she was able to resist?

Yeah, not so long.

"Come on, Peaches." He closed the distance between them, cupping her chin with one hand while guiding her hips toward him with the other. "The boy wants you to stay."

"This is a terrible idea. We don't want to give him the wrong impression of our relationship."

"What kind of impression? I didn't say you could sleep in my bed!" He feigned shock with his mouth wide open and a devilish glint in his eyes. "We'll make a giant bed on the living room floor, watch some movies, eat some junk food. Joey can't stay up too late because he has to get up for school in the morning. I'm not even on call tonight. You can be on one side, I'll be on the other. But if you can't stay away from me—and I know it will be difficult for you—we could maybe sneak into the other room once he's sleeping."

"You're crazy."

"You know you want to."

"Do not!" She lied.

Why was the idea so appealing? She was a loner. A solitary wolf. She *avoided* children like one would avoid peanuts if they had an allergy. She certainly didn't voluntarily stay overnight with them.

"You know you want to stay with me." He lifted

her chin and captured her lips with his own.

How was she supposed to argue when she couldn't even think around him?

"You're staying?" Joey's cheerful screech startled her, making her jump away in shame. "Daddy, you cheated. You're not supposed to *kiss* her. Yuck. She's a *girl*, you know!"

Quentin threw up his hands in surrender. "I know, I know. It was a moment of weakness. I'll try not to do it again. But you wanted me to convince her, didn't you?"

"She likes kisses?"

"She likes *my* kisses."

Joey scrunched up his face in disgust while Savannah rolled her eyes at Quentin's lack of humility.

Joey pushed Quentin out of the way and wrapped his arms around Savannah's waist. She couldn't lie—her heart became a puddle. His hug was as brief as his calm. He dragged her across the room and started barking orders at her as he directed the slumber party set-up.

She complied, behaving like an obedient soldier.

Quentin moved the furniture out of the way and brought another pile of blankets from his room.

"I'll tell Nana Robby she can take the rest of the night off." Quentin winked over Joey's head, making mush of Savannah's knees. "She stays in the in-law apartment downstairs. She usually uses her own entrance when she's not working."

A fleet of helium balloons took flight in Savannah's belly and her heart.

Not Over You

Not even halfway through the movie, Joey was sound asleep.

"I can't believe he snores so loud."

"He doesn't get that from me," Quentin smirked, watching Savannah from the corner of his eye.

"Yeah, right. Don't pretend I've never heard you sleep."

She threw a pillow at him. He caught it easily.

"Ah, so a pillow fight is what you want, eh?" His smile was wicked. Seductive. Deadly.

"Don't you dare. You'll wake him up!"

"An elephant dancing on his forehead wouldn't wake him up now." Quentin crawled predatorily toward her, carefully avoiding Joey. "Come with me. We'll take this fight into my room."

Savannah grabbed a handful of popcorn and stuffed it into her mouth. Speaking around the white cheddar stuff, she said, "I have to see what happens to that poor robot."

"I'll tell you later."

Quentin stood, pulling her up with him.

Breathing him in, she couldn't think of one single reason why she shouldn't give in to her impulses.

She couldn't even convince herself that she didn't deserve this.

In his eyes, she was so much more than she thought she could ever be. And with his hands glued to the side of her face and his eyes hypnotizing her, she could almost believe her value.

She opened her mouth to argue, but his finger covered it as he whispered, "Shhhh."

She nibbled on his finger, looking up at him through eyes that were growing heavy with the need to be with him.

He pulled her close, kissing her deeply as he walked her toward his room.

With one foot, he kicked the door closed, leaving Rocco on the other side. Rocco whined once, then must have given up, because she didn't hear him again.

"Quentin..."

"No talking." He made it impossible to get any words out, anyway. He kept her tongue occupied in the most delicious way.

"I..."

"We can talk all you want later." He kissed her collarbone, nibbling gently as he started lifting her shirt. "Right now I have a different kind of conversation in mind."

His playfulness turned to a serious commitment to turning her into a walking orgasm in milliseconds.

They fell to the bed together, his weight pressing her into the bed. If she had to be crushed, there was no more delicious way for it to happen.

His erection pressed into her thigh. She lifted her legs and wrapped them around his waist, shifting his hardness over to her softness. They had to lose the clothes before she lost her mind.

He wouldn't allow her to rush things, though. Oh, no. He clearly had other plans.

She managed to get his shirt over his head before he pinned her hands to the bed above her. With his free hand, he traced a finger over every one of her curves that he could reach. Her shoulder. Her breast. Her hard, pointy nipple. Over her ribs. Around her belly button. Along the curve of her hip.

He dragged his finger slowly, torturously over her belly, drawing an imaginary line from one hipbone to the other. A wildfire threatened to burn the place down if he didn't stop fanning the flames. Or, more accurately, a flood was about to occur.

She struggled to free her hands, needing to feel his flexing muscles.

Ten years had passed since she had been this excited. This full of life. This—dare she say it?—happy.

Quentin made her happy. No use denying it.

And she wanted them to be *happy* together. Now.

She tore her hands out of his grasp and jumped off the bed, ready to put an end to the torment. Or to move it into more dangerous territory. His eyes brightened with the kind of delight that made her belly burn. His smile turned wicked when she shimmied out of her pants and panties, not taking her eyes off his. She stood still, bare and naked, sweaty and seduced. Waiting. Waiting. Waiting.

His Adam's apple enlarged as he stared at her, drinking her in. She remained still, a tall glass of wine, filled to the brim with the need to intoxicate him.

As he had intoxicated her.

She watched as more than desire charged his energy.

He was remembering. Just as she could never forget.

Quentin Elliott was her first love. Her only love.

The only man who had ever made her feel that she was worth anything.

He had been the one from the "bad" family, but he had always been capable of rising above and soaring over the others.

Quentin had always been free about declaring his love for her. He had made his plans clear—he would marry her. He would take care of her. He would be her anchor in a crazy world.

And she had tossed it all away. She had left him, never considering that he may have wanted her to stay.

"Whoa, what's happening here?" Quentin rushed to stand, cupping her face between his powerful hands and jumping into the depths of her eyes, not knowing the danger he leapt to. Never considering how he could get hurt.

She had devoted enough time to sorrow. To pain.

Now was the time to pay him back for being the one good thing in her life.

She blinked away whatever negativity he had seen and shifted back into gear. Her body was making demands, and if she didn't follow through…

Her eyelids lowered and he accepted her unspoken invitation.

His tongue met hers, immediately returning her to the height of passion. She would dive headfirst off the cliff if he was waiting below.

And she was ready to do it now.

She inhaled deeply as their kisses grew more urgent. His smell was her fuel. No matter how much time passed, breathing in his scent was like smelling grandma's cookies—only hotter. She was transported back to a simpler time, a time when the worst thing she had done was to stay out past curfew or to get a D in math class. When the most exciting thing was seeing Quentin naked for the first time and wondering how on earth he'd fit that thing in her.

But he had managed to fit before, and she couldn't *wait* to fit together again.

Her hands slid down his torso until she reached his pants. She fumbled for a moment, but he moved in for the assist.

When they were both gloriously—oh, so gloriously!—naked, she took a moment to take it all in.

But not too long of a moment, because his erection waved her on, urging her to touch, to stroke, to devour.

There was so much she wanted to do. But when he placed his hands on her waist and pulled her close, she lost control and leapt onto him, knocking him back onto the bed.

He had tiny laugh lines around his eyes that she promptly kissed. While she did that, he cupped her breasts, pressing them together, then moving down to kiss and lick and suck each tip as she arched her back and grabbed his head.

When she knew she couldn't wait any longer, she reached over to her pants pocket and retrieved a condom. She lifted herself enough to access him and dressed him for the occasion. Without another thought, she slowly, carefully, eagerly lowered herself onto him, taking each inch with the care it deserved.

His breathing quickened and his eyes darkened. His hand on her butt helped guide her movements as she thrust against him. She rolled her pelvis, evoking a massive eyes-up-in-his-head moment that made her hotter than a preheated oven as she took him as deep as he would go.

"You're so fucking hot," Quentin growled, nibbling the top of her breast as sweat poured out of him. She rarely heard him swear, but hearing his voice turn so raw and demanding—her sweet, gentle Quentin—drove her nearly to the brink of explosion.

She quickened her pace, her breasts bouncing in his face.

He tweaked her nipple as she struggled not to scream.

They found their release at the same moment. The same beautiful, loving, delectable moment. She shuddered—actually shuddered—as a series of orgasms rippled through her before sending her back without a parachute.

She panted against his chest as she struggled to regain some semblance of grace.

He rubbed her back and seemed to struggle to do the same.

"You're even hotter than you were as a teen," he muttered, lifting her chin so she'd face him.

She smiled, but had no words to add.

But hell yeah—he had always been hot, even as an awkward teen boy. Desirable. Girls had always tried to steal him from her.

Not Over You

But he was more now than anything she had ever imagined a man could be.

And for the first time in a decade, she was content to leave her running shoes by the door.

Chapter Thirteen

Savannah floated back home. Not really, but she certainly *felt* like clouds of bliss carried her. Rocco walked with a lighter step, too, probably picking up on her uncharacteristically positive energy.

She smiled, then grimaced, then smiled again when she realized there'd been a lot of that uncharacteristic energy coming from her lately.

The morning had been almost as perfect as the delightfully sleepless night. After the most fantastic lovemaking session of her life, they had snuck back out to the living room so they'd be in their appropriate spots before Joey woke up.

She laughed as she remembered Joey bouncing out of his sleeping bag as if he had never stopped to sleep. He dragged his dad and Savannah into the kitchen. Joey had dragged the stool to various cabinets, pulling out things he knew they'd need to make pancakes.

Quentin had tried to insist that Savannah not be allowed to cook, but Joey came to her defense.

Together, they whipped up two batches of

pancakes—one blueberry, one chocolate chip. Savannah impressed Joey with her ability to make funky shapes on the frying pan. His last words as he rushed out the door for his daddy to take him to school were, "Next time can you make a car?"

Quentin had snuck back in after getting Joey buckled into his seat. His kisses were urgent, desperate. She had clung to him at first, but then had to push him out the door so Joey wouldn't be late to school.

Her body began to burn. Mostly in her heart region.

"Oh, Rocco. What have we gotten ourselves into?"

He barked in response. If only he could give her the answers. He had been her greatest ally and supporter for two years now. He'd know how she should proceed. She wished he could tell her.

After cleaning up the kitchen, she had drawn a heart on a napkin and left it on the counter. She had let herself out knowing that Quentin had to work after dropping off Joey.

She quickened her pace, wanting to get to the studio so she could change into running clothes.

The test results for the bone marrow donation would be in today. Her nerves were zinging with anxiety, so exercise was essential.

Her mind drifted to a dark place. A place where she was a failure and let people down. A place where she was a killer—not a rescuer.

With a giant rush of unexpected self-esteem, she shoved those thoughts to the deep recesses of her mind.

Things were going great—way better than she expected. She knew all the way to her toes that the results would be positive. It was her mother, after all. They were blood related. They'd match.

Savannah would be able to help her mother heal physically after taking so much from her emotionally.

A tiny portion of her unspoken debt would be repaid.

The colors around her were suddenly brighter with this new revelation. The green leaves glimmered. The blue sky beamed. Even the brown on the forest floor appeared golden.

The world smiled.

Savannah smiled back.

And then her phone rang.

Her mind shut down when she heard the doctor's apology.

She was not a match.

***

Savannah threw things. Then she cleaned things. Then she packed up her duffel bag.

Last time she had left without a word. This time she had to be a grown-up and apologize appropriately.

She couldn't trust herself to do it in person, so she did what she thought was best. She wrote letters.

Her letter to her stepfather was heartfelt. Deeply apologetic. She knew she owed him so much. She knew she was shattering his heart by leaving this way. But she'd hurt him more if she stayed. How would he look at her every day, knowing that she was unable to help in the one way they had all hoped she would?

Hurting was what she did. Hadn't life been proving that to her all along?

Her letter to her mother had her choking on emotion that begged to be expressed. She couldn't stand the thought that she hadn't been able to help her mother. This was supposed to be the way she, in some small way, made up for letting Brandon die.

What kind of daughter wasn't a match for her own mother?

Praying wasn't normally her go-to method of solving problems, but she got down on her knees and said a prayer to whatever higher power would listen, begging someone—anyone—to spare her mother and take her instead.

Her mother had suffered enough.

Her last letter was to Joey. She kept it light—thanking him for making her feel so welcome, for including her in their fun, and for being such a wonderful spirit.

She had to write it twice because teardrops smeared the first version.

She started to write to Quentin. She couldn't continue. There were no words that could explain what he meant to her. There were no words that could make up for what she had done. There were no words that could make him think better of her.

So she drew a heart on a paper and folded it up

tight.

She prayed that he got the message that she tried to emblazon on the paper. The message her heart so desperately wanted to send.

She even allowed the teardrops to stain his paper. This way he wouldn't doubt her feelings.

***

Quentin stopped into Cup-A-Plenty Café for a quick dose of caffeine. Though, truthfully, every muscle in his body revved with excitement at the memory of last night. He had a feeling he'd be on alert all day even if he hadn't slept a bit.

He gripped his cup tighter as he tried to walk casually onto Main Street. Anytime his thoughts turned to Savannah, his walk became more challenging as his pants became tighter.

Steps away from his truck, Quentin's attention was drawn to the doorway of Miss Molly's shop. He'd recognize that tight ass anywhere, and he wasn't referring to Miss Molly's.

Rocco broke free of Savannah's grasp and ran for Quentin. Quentin opened his arms and invited the dog to jump onto him, much to the chagrin of his owner.

Savannah's apparent panic at Rocco's escape soon gave way to a look of irritation when she noticed Rocco's wayward jumping. She scolded Rocco, forcing the dog onto all four legs. If the dog had a tail, Quentin was certain it would have been tucked between his legs. Quentin could empathize—he had been on the receiving end of that look a time or two.

Like now.

Quentin cleared his throat, choked back his laughter, and joked about sending her his dry cleaning bill, even though they both knew Rocco only jumped by invitation.

Savannah turned back toward Miss Molly, fidgeting with the cuff of her sweatshirt.

She shifted from one foot to the other, looking over her shoulder as if hoping he wouldn't still be there.

He stepped forward, placing his hand on her lower back.

She jumped.

Miss Molly looked back and forth between the two of them, shaking her head and drawing her lips in over her false teeth.

"I really thought the two of you would give it a go. Can't say I'm not disappointed."

Huh?

Savannah leaned forward, leaving his hand dangling awkwardly in the air. Rocco happily took her place, enjoying Quentin's administrations.

Savannah hugged Miss Molly. Questions raced through his head. Why did it feel like they were saying goodbye?

Savannah pulled away without a word and started walking down the street—away from Miss Molly and away from him.

He looked to Miss Molly for a clue. She didn't say anything either. She simply walked back into her shop, grabbing a broom as she went.

"Savannah?"

He jogged to catch up, tossing his still-full coffee cup in a trash barrel.

His hand on her arm stopped her. She turned and smiled. To a casual observer, she looked happy. Normal. Pleased to see him.

But he could see the aura of sadness in her eyes. Fewer smile lines on her face than she had when full of unadulterated joy. The kind she had last night.

"What's wrong?" He grasped her arms with both of his hands, studying her for a sign. "Is everyone okay?" He would have heard if something had happened to her mother—he was on shift.

She blinked too fast, then began rubbing her chest with the heel of her palm.

"Peaches, you only rub your heart when something is hurting you. Let me help you."

She dropped her hand to his arm, and then stepped into his embrace. Her head rested on his chest as he wrapped his arms around her, holding tight. He'd chase away whatever demons fought their way into her mind.

"You're not alone."

She returned the hug, clutching him tighter than she ever had before. He kissed the top of her head.

"Come on, let me get you a coffee."

"I can't, but thanks. Rocco and I were just getting ready to go for a run."

She wasn't wearing her running clothes, and her hair wasn't in a ponytail. He knew damn well she hated running on concrete.

Beads of sweat gathered at his temples. He caught himself holding his breath.

"Savannah." His voice held a note of warning. Of unexplained terror. She pulled away and couldn't meet his eyes.

He had thought this awkward push-pull was behind them after last night. Not just the sex, but the peace. The relaxation. The ease in which they related to one another.

He thought they were on the same page. Openly.

So why was she pulling away emotionally? What could he have possibly done wrong?

He opened his mouth to ask the questions that plagued his mind, but his cell buzzed with an alert. Great. Perfect timing for an emergency.

"Shit."

Savannah raised her eyebrows in question.

"Look, there's an emergency. Please wait here. I need to talk to you."

She smiled, but the way she sucked the corner of her lower lip into her teeth didn't leave him feeling confident.

"Please."

God damn it all. His voice cracked like a fucking toddler's.

His phone buzzed again.

He started to back away toward his truck, but he couldn't bring himself to turn around. He didn't want to give her the opportunity to bolt.

She held her hand up in the saddest goodbye he had ever witnessed. It didn't feel like she was saying "see ya later." Her raised hand and watery eyes had a ring of finality that he couldn't explain.

He closed his eyes, blew a kiss, then shifted into paramedic gear, convincing himself that he was just being an insecure asshole. There was no reason she'd truly pull away. He was overthinking things. Lack of sleep. Low blood sugar. High paranoia.

Things would be okay.

***

Things would not be okay.

Savannah cursed and hit the steering wheel as she turned onto the highway, leaving Healing Springs behind.

She didn't dare look in her rear view mirror. She was too afraid she'd be pulled back.

She swiped at tears that refused to stop rolling down her cheeks. Ten years of not crying and now she was a leaky faucet? Unacceptable.

Even Rocco didn't know what to make of it all. He had sniffed around her, licked the tears on the right side of her face, then forced his way to the back seat where he did his best to get comfortable on the seat.

As if on cue, clouds moved in, reducing her visibility and helping to remind her that sunny days didn't really exist. They had been a figment of her imagination. Easy to forget.

She'd return to her old life and be just fine.

She had done this before. She could do it again.

She just had to stop thinking of everything she left behind. All the hearts she wanted to be part of. All the forgiveness she had been granted.

She hadn't even been able to give her mother the one little thing she should have been able to give.

She was a failure. Always was. Always would be.

Quentin and Joey hadn't seen her that way. But they would. Quentin was a *healer* for crying out loud. He had chosen a profession where he could help the most people. When he found out that she wasn't even qualified to donate bone marrow to her ailing mother, he'd never be able to think of her as his equal.

Joey had somehow managed to bond with Savannah's mother—something Savannah herself had never managed to do. How would he feel if the woman died? What about the inevitable day when small-town rumors reached his young ears and told him the truth? Of how Savannah Grace had killed her brother *and* her mother?

Yeah, better for her to hightail it out of there before any more attachments could be made.

Joey would forget about her.

And she'd hold on to the brief moments when she had been loved.

She'd carry the hugs and sweet words with her forever. Because even though she didn't deserve them, no one could take the memories away.

Amanda Torrey

***

Quentin backhanded the pile of mail off the side of the kitchen island, swearing and pacing around the kitchen.

How dare his ex petition for joint custody of *his* son? She hadn't had any contact in years, and now she thought she should serve him with papers?

Not happening.

Nana Robby entered the room just as he was releasing some of his more potent words.

"I guess this is a bad time." But she didn't retreat.

"Sorry, Robby. Bad news in the mail."

"I'm afraid I have something that might make your day a little worse." She extended her arm, holding some folded, lined papers toward him. "I'll take Joey to the park for a while after school so you have some time to decompress. Dinner is all set, but if you prefer to go out for the evening, I will put Joey to bed."

Quentin mumbled his thanks, appreciating that Nana Robby always knew when she was most needed.

He retreated to his study, where a desk full of sticky notes reminded him he had to contact various people to be sure the Tree House project was still on track.

Quentin settled into his chair. His mind didn't quite register what he was reading. It was addressed to Joey, but it was in Savannah's handwriting.

And then he opened the other paper. A giant heart, one that matched the one she had left on the napkin in the kitchen. The one he had smiled at before opening the mail. The one he had thought meant he was indeed crazy and everything was just fine.

This heart was smudged in parts with what could only be teardrops.

This heart didn't represent the beginning of something, as he had thought the one in the kitchen had. This one represented the end of something.

Quentin crumpled up both papers and tossed them across the room.

He was all set with women.

And he badly needed a drink.

***

Savannah left her bag in the car. She'd get it later. Rocco happily rushed off to his favorite spot to pee.

She shook her head when she noticed Valentina's statue of St. Anthony standing outside, his stony face turned to the wall. He normally took the place of honor on the shelf behind the check-out area.

"There's my girl!" Valentina rushed over with her arms open, her large hips sashaying and her huge skirt threatening to pull things off the shelves. Savannah buried her face in Valentina's comforting shoulder, absorbing the comfort and feeling grateful to be home. "Tell me all about it."

"First you have to tell me why St. Anthony is outside."

Valentina narrowed her eyes toward the door, pushing her chin up and adjusting her shoulders. "He knows what he did."

Savannah laughed at the older woman's eccentricity. She'd actually fit in quite nicely in Healing Springs.

"I saw that storm cloud pass over your eyes. Don't you dare try to hide anything from me, little miss."

Savannah tightened her lips. She couldn't talk about it.

"Savannah Grace. I have known you for ten years. I have never seen your eyes red and puffy before. Not even once. Don't make me put you out there with St. Anthony. You tell me what has you lookin' like that disaster of a strawberry cake I made."

A smile forced its way onto Savannah's face. Tempted to open up and spill everything, she was saved by the ringing of the bells on the door as a customer came in.

Valentina rushed over to the door. "I'm very sorry, Trudy, but you'll have to come back. We're closed for a short break." Valentina gently shoved the frequent browser out of the shop, then flipped the sign to the "Closed" position. She locked the deadbolt and turned back toward a shocked Savannah.

"Don't look so surprised. You're my girl, and something happened. Spill."

So Savannah did. She told her about Joey and Quentin and her car crash and fixing up the studio and finding the boxes of memories and the worry jar and the impending graduation and her failed attempt at making a muffin. Everything. Things that mattered, things that didn't. Savannah had no way of filtering what was important from what wasn't. It was all one big memory. Indecipherable.

Savannah paced up and down the aisle, waving her hands in the air, desperate to articulate everything.

She was in the beginning of telling her about Rocco's response to country music when Valentina put her plump hands on Savannah's arms, stilling her and effectively putting an end to the recap of events.

"Tell me this, my girl. Are you a match? For your mama?"

Savannah felt her eyes widen, her breath quicken, and her heart rate revving up enough to launch a nuclear missile.

She shook her head, then lost control of her muscles.

Her body began to slink to the floor, but Valentina kept her upright.

"Baby girl, you've been trying to be too strong for too long. There's strength in letting go, too, you know."

Savannah could say nothing. She'd be learning to let go all over again. She could have her PhD in letting go.

Valentina smoothed Savannah's hair, puffy from the ocean-side humidity. She led Savannah over to the window seat, settling her in amongst the mismatched throw pillows. Savannah inched her way into the corner, grabbing the biggest pillow to clutch to her belly. She felt young, vulnerable.

She didn't like it.

"Honey, didn't they tell you the probability was

very low for the match? When my family went through something like this, they cautioned us that only something like thirty percent of family members would be a match. But they can find someone else. She's in the donor bank, right?"

Savannah nodded.

Thirty percent? That would have been freaking nice to know. She wouldn't have allowed her hopes to be raised for thirty percent odds!

"They didn't tell you, did they? Oh, girl." Valentina brushed hair out of Savannah's face. "They'll find a way."

Savannah wasn't convinced. Her luck didn't work that way.

"In the meantime, you regaled me with many a tale of a certain man. Now you were never one to talk about your past, but I'm guessin' that man was a part of it. I'm thinkin' you shouldn't have left so quickly. I bet he's waiting with open arms for you."

"No, that's over. I broke it."

"Can't break love, my girl. Go back. There's nothing here for you. It's all there."

"You're here."

"Oh, honey. If that were enough, I wouldn't be pushing you out the door. Truth is, you're a daughter to me. But I've kept you to myself long enough. You have another family who needs you. I need you to honor that."

"Valentina, I can't—"

"Hush now, my girl. I'm not going to push you out. You'll always have a home here. But did you even say goodbye to your mama?"

Savannah pressed her cold hands to her hot cheeks.

"You didn't. Okay, well I'm not gonna lie. That would be heartbreaking to a mother. I want you to give that some thought."

Savannah hugged the pillow closer. She *couldn't* say goodbye. Her mother wouldn't have wanted to hear from her, anyway. Valentina didn't know Savannah's mother. She didn't know how cold and disconnected she could be. She didn't know the dark, tumultuous energy that swirled around her. She didn't know that Savannah was not the only one who believed the wrong sibling had died.

"Listen, I've got to open up this shop before old Trudy has a nutty. You go on and take a nap or watch some TV or whatever it is your little heart needs to do. Go on into my apartment if you want to take a Jacuzzi tubby. We'll get things figured out later."

Savannah could feel the remnants of a lipstick kiss on her forehead even as she trudged to the back of the shop toward her apartment.

"Before you close that door, let me tell you something my auntie used to tell me. She said that being a mother is the hardest job on the planet. Now you know I never had kids—I buried every one of the poor little souls I tried to birth—but there's nothin' in the world I'd want more than to have my daughter with me. No matter what she'd done, I'd want her to forgive herself."

Savannah tried to respond, but her throat felt as

though she had swallowed sticky glue, and Valentina had gone to open the door, anyway. So she closed her apartment door and plopped herself onto her bed, shoulders slumped, completely dejected.

She had been fine when she left here.

Her life had been in order. She'd had Valentina and Rocco and no other concerns.

Life had been great.

She looked closer. Her possessions could fit into one box—she had accumulated almost nothing over the last decade. No ticket stubs. No collectable items. No photos of friends or family. From this vantage point, her life looked pretty empty. She'd actually be embarrassed if anyone entered this room.

It was clean as a museum, but with nothing to show for the time she had spent here.

Savannah whipped off her clothes, not wanting to wear anything associated with her last day in Healing Springs. She could still smell Quentin on her shirt—his scent drifted back to her as she tossed the clothing into the laundry hamper.

She splashed cold water on her face and dressed in running clothes. Rocco perked his head up as she slipped into an old pair of sneakers she hadn't gotten around to throwing away. Slipping back into her old life felt *good*.

She ignored the gnawing sensation of emptiness in her gut.

Before she left the room, she retrieved the shirt she had been wearing—the one with Quentin's scent clinging to it—and tucked it under her pillow, refusing

Not Over You

to question her motives.

She closed her eyes when she reached the beach, taking in every sensation and willing it to be enough.

***

Quentin had done everything over the past few days to keep his mind off the atrocities of women. He had picked up extra shifts. He had taken Joey to every park within a fifteen-mile radius. He had spent late nights drinking with his buddy, Cole, who was crashing in town for a few days in between projects.

He only had one thing left to do.

Put the house on the market.

Cole had tried to get him to wait for a bit—to give his head time to catch up to his heart. Or vice versa. He couldn't remember what shit Cole had been flinging, but none of it made sense to him.

Yeah, he loved Savannah. She knew it. He even allowed himself to believe she had feelings for him, too.

He could forgive the fact that she had left him after Brandon's death. That was about her—not him. He got it.

But this time?

It shouldn't matter what she was going through. She knew he was here. She knew he could help. She didn't want him to. She didn't want *him*.

"Don't let what's happening with Merry affect

how you feel about Savvy." Cole's wisdom, divvied out between shots, only managed to piss Quentin off. Why the hell shouldn't one affect the other? There had to have been some kind of fucking oath women took to mess with a man any way they could.

He tried to be one of the good guys. Didn't women always bitch that there were no good guys left?

Lotta good it did him.

"Did I tell you that your old girl is Joey's kindergarten teacher?" Quentin had appreciated the death look he got from Cole and the subsequent double shot they had each tossed down. "Did I also mention she's happily engaged? Sucks to be you, huh?"

"Fuck you." Cole had ordered another round and requested that the bartender keep 'em coming.

Quentin swallowed ibuprofen as he filed the affidavit with the court the next day. No way was he letting Merry have joint custody. If she was lucky, maybe he'd let her have supervised visits. Only if it would benefit Joey.

And no way would he let Savannah live in his memory any longer. He had bought the house because he was stupid and in love, even then. He had mistakenly believed he could get her back one day. That they could heal together. That she'd be thrilled to learn the lengths he had gone to make her happy, even in her absence.

Those days were long fucking gone. He'd sell the house and buy a new one with his own specifications in mind. Maybe he'd even move to the city. She'd hate that.

He dropped his head into his hands.

What was he thinking?

She'd never even know the outcome.

This was something he had to do for himself. He had to sell the house to rid himself of her memory. He and Joey and Nana Robby would pick out something suitable. Something perfect. For them. Not for the ghost of the past.

He didn't need an exorcist to rid himself of any lingering feelings he may be carrying around for her. All he needed was the memory of her leaving without saying a word to him. Of letting him hold her in his arms, all while planning to tear his pathetic heart out of his chest and leave it thumping for her on Main Street.

He had never known such anger. He'd never hurt her, but he sure as hell hoped he never had to see her again.

Chapter Fourteen

She had to see him again.

She was crazy. She was stupid. She was lost.

And she was in love.

Her morning run on the beach with Rocco had turned into a sprint as she rushed back to the shop to share the news with Valentina. After a full week of living in denial, she couldn't go one more day without resting her head on his shoulder. Without breathing his scent—the fresh scent, not the rapidly-fading, stuck-to-the-T-shirt scent she was settling for. She needed him to know that he meant more to her than anything else in the world. More than the grief she stubbornly refused to deal with. More than the pain of being in that town, surrounded by memories. More than her selfish desire to wallow in the pain, to torment herself for reasons she now realized weren't very smart.

She ran faster. Faster than she had ever thought possible.

More than her knees ached when she was hit by the realization that she couldn't run forever.

And she needed to make things right with her mother and stepfather.

This morning, Savannah had received a message from her stepfather. A donor had been found for Mom. Some anonymous person from the donor bank.

Savannah reached and reached for a word that would describe her gratitude, but none existed. Pieces of the guilt that had been weighing her down floated out into the ocean air. She still wished it could be her giving her mother the life-saving treatment, but since it couldn't be, she said a prayer of gratitude that this donor had matched. And a prayer of intention that she would be present as her mother went through the procedures. She would be there to help her mother heal, even if Savannah didn't feel one hundred percent worthy or wanted.

After days of missing Quentin and Joey and her stupid hometown and nights of crying herself to sleep listening to sappy music, Savannah had gained some insight.

She had been selfish. She hadn't been punishing only herself, she had been punishing everyone who had ever known or loved her. Keeping herself closed off emotionally, running at every sign of trouble, allowing fear to rule her life. She was shocked that Quentin had given her as many chances as he had.

She didn't know if she would have it in her to be so open-minded if she had been in his position.

She had been so blind to her pain that she hadn't been able to see the love that was being given so freely to her.

She hadn't earned his love, but she swore to every higher power who would listen that she'd spend the rest of her life working toward being worthy.

Savannah burst through the door of the shop, startling Valentina and her customer, but possibly startling herself even more. Impulsivity was not part of her usual repertoire. But her mind was made up. She just had to be sure Valentina was okay with it.

Savannah paced the small area near her handmade jewelry display while she waited for Valentina to finish ringing out the elderly couple. Rocco, exhausted from the extra exertion, spread out on his back in front of their apartment door at the rear of the shop. Savannah chuckled at the vision of his giant tongue nearly reaching the floor and his paws all pointing toward the ceiling. Didn't look too comfy, but to each his own.

"You're going back to him, aren't you, Savvy girl?"

Savannah cocked her head at Valentina, reminding herself of her dog when he was trying to figure her out.

"How did you—"

"It's written all over you, my girl." Valentina scuttled around the checkout counter, arms wide. "Come and give me a hug."

Savannah stepped into Valentina's loving embrace, squeezing tight. "I'm sorry that I'm all sweaty."

Valentina laughed. "I'm proud of you."

Was she really? Savannah stepped back, studying the face of the woman who took her in all those years ago and made her part of her family.

She wouldn't leave her in the lurch. No matter how much she needed to be with Quentin, she couldn't turn her back on Valentina. She owed her everything.

"Are you sure this is okay? I won't leave here if you still need me. Honest. I can do a long distance thing or—"

"Stop right there. Do I look like a killer of true love? I'm named Valentina, for crying out loud. Romance is practically in my blood. You will go there and make me proud. Just don't forget to invite me to the wedding."

Savannah pressed her hot hands to her hotter cheeks. She didn't know if a wedding would be in her future, but if so, she'd want Valentina to be there.

But why did her chest tighten so painfully at the thought of leaving Valentina and everything this coastal town represented?

"What's the matter, my precious?"

Valentina had always been able to sense when something was bothering Savannah. Lying would be of no use, because Valentina had a way of seeing through Savannah, too.

"I feel bad leaving."

Valentina grabbed Savannah's arms and gently squeezed.

"Oh, honey. I won't be hanging around here forever. Matter of fact, I've been wanting to get out of here for a long time. I've stayed because you've needed me. Now that you don't, I'll move along in life. I've got the traveling bug in my bones. I'm ready to sell this place just as soon as you're ready to be on your own. I'm thinkin' you know where your rightful place is."

"You're selling?"

"Oh, don't look so surprised. You've seen the brochures I've kept stashed away back there. I've been working hard for years—time to go spend some of that hard-earned cash on a cruise or two."

"I've always seen you as more of an RVer."

"Yeah, well maybe that, too, when I get back from the Bahamas. Who knows? I'm just glad I won't have to worry about my girl while I'm gone. I'll be able to picture you living in bliss with the man of your heart."

"Have I been holding you back from living your dreams, Val? I've never intended to do that! I'm a big girl—you could have gone anytime."

"You held me back from *nothin'*. You've given me more joy than anything else in this world. You'll always be my girl. I'm just happy you're able to leave the nest and land in a comfy place." Valentina touched Savannah's cheek in a maternal gesture. "What's this? Tears? In all the years I've known you, girl, you've never shed a tear."

Savannah gulped hard, closed her eyes, and shook her head. She had so much she wanted to say, but it was all trapped behind the brick wall in her throat.

"Go get your pretty little runner's butt packing. I want you out of here by the end of the week. Time for me to get this place sold and start travelin' the world while I've still got the ability to do so."

As new customers rushed in, Savannah closed the

door on her past and prepared to move on into her future.

***

Everything she owned had fit into the trunk and backseat of her car, which should have been depressing if not for the realization that she would be building a new life with a fresh start. With Quentin.

Or so she hoped.

She wanted to surprise him by showing up in Healing Springs, but she had tried to call and text him just to chat. To apologize for leaving the way she did.

He never answered or replied.

It wasn't like him to get mad at her; he was probably busy. He worked a lot and spent every second he could doing fun things with Joey.

Quentin was *perfect*.

She imagined his sculpted arms wrapped around her. His callused hands stoking a fire within her. His lips turning into a grin before working their own magic on her. His flawless good looks and his endless humility— or sometimes, his lack of it. His need to help others— to heal even the most broken. The kind of loving, involved father he was. His dedication to his entire community.

He was too good for her, but luckily for her, he hadn't seemed to have figured that out.

After all these years, Quentin had welcomed her back into his life. His love was as strong for her as hers had been for him. Fate was her very best friend.

The stupid smile wouldn't go away. She felt like an idiot driving down the highway with a giant grin on her face.

Clearly Rocco thought she was an idiot, too, if his grunt was any indication. But when she rolled the window down for him to stick his head out into the wind, he wore the same smile.

Savannah admired the signs and special landscaping decorating the town in honor of their high school graduation.

Brandon would have been graduating this year, too.

Several weeks ago, this thought would have slayed her. She wouldn't have been able to deal.

But now, thanks in large part to Quentin, she was able to acknowledge the sadness while still appreciating the beauty of every day.

Savannah had planned to stop in to see her parents first, but she couldn't keep her heart from taking the wheel and demanding that she find the other half of the aching organ first.

Rocco became more animated as they turned onto the road that would lead to Quentin's Victorian-on-the-lake.

Even he knew where they belonged.

Savannah took a deep breath of the fresh pine air and tried to steady her nerves. Positive visualization was supposed to be a powerful thing, right? She visualized an overjoyed Quentin rushing toward her, arms ready to catch her, eager to drag her into his bed.

Not Over You

Oh, wait, on a Saturday morning, Joey would be home. The bed would have to wait for later. But maybe she could sneak in a kiss or two, and then they could take Joey to do something fun.

Magical things were about to happen.

There he was.

At the end of his gravel driveway.

With his back to her, she had a moment to appreciate the beauty of his fine, tight ass—just begging to be squeezed.

She admired his biceps as he swung a sledgehammer onto some sort of wooden pole. Looked like he was putting up a sign, but she couldn't tell what it said.

He must have finally heard the car, because he turned around, giving her a full view of his scowl, his scruffy beard, and the For Sale sign on the front lawn.

Chapter Fifteen

If his body didn't stop reacting to the devil pulling into the driveway, he'd take the hammer to his own damned foot.

Quentin deepened his scowl and leaned casually on the sign, hoping he looked like he meant it.

He gave no weight to the fact that his heart was thudding so loud he could no longer hear her car engine. The tightening of his zipper was purely coincidental. And the fact that he wanted to run over and rip her out of the car so he could twirl her around in a dance of ecstasy clearly meant he needed an anti-psychotic.

Or to grow a pair.

What the hell did she want now? She had put his heart through the meat grinder—wasn't that enough? Or did she come to shovel up what was left of the sludge so she could feed it to the local pigs?

He wouldn't give her the chance to hurt him again.

Dammit, why was he reduced to the emotions of a

Not Over You

teenager when she was around?

He had to hurry and get her out of here before Joey came home. Nana Robby had taken him to get a haircut in preparation for the graduation this afternoon. He didn't need to see her and get a false sense of hope. He hadn't understood why she took off the way she did, and Quentin didn't want to have to continue making excuses for her.

His scowl didn't chase her off. She had the nerve to get out of the car. One tanned, sculpted leg at a time.

Shit.

He cleared his throat and narrowed his eyes.

She walked toward him anyway. He fought to keep his eyes locked on hers rather than on her toned belly and slender hips, showed off to goddamned perfection in her half-shirt and low-rise cut-off short shorts. Were outfits like those invented just to make men do stupid things?

He wouldn't succumb.

"Hey."

Her voice was as shaky as he figured his would be. He didn't try to find out.

"I guess you've been busy." He watched her throat move as she swallowed. She began to fiddle with the collar on her shirt. The urge to replace her hand with his and to tear the shirt away from her tempting skin was strong.

But he wouldn't succumb.

He tightened his grip on the sledgehammer instead.

"You're selling the house?"

He nodded. Once. That was all she'd get from him.

"Why? You never mentioned that to me."

No. He hadn't mentioned it to her. And he wouldn't explain himself now.

He turned away and resumed his hammering. He'd make sure that sign didn't go anywhere.

He closed his eyes when her arms looped around his waist. Her head rested on his back. He wanted to push her away. To swear at her. To tell her he wished she had never come back in the first place. To tell her she wasn't welcome in this town ever again.

All he could do was force his body to stiffen. To not melt into her. To be a man, dammit!

"I'd like to make an offer." Her words vibrated on his back, sending chills down his spine. "On the house, of course."

He tossed the hammer to the side and turned, holding her at arm's length.

"What do you want from me? Why are you here?" His growl didn't frighten her away like he hoped. It seemed to have made her shoulders straighten and her chin point upward.

"I told you. I want to make an offer on the house. With one stipulation."

Yeah, there was always a stipulation. Did she want him to leave his bloody heart—what was left of it—on the counter?

"I must insist that all occupants stay."

"I'm not selling for the money, Savannah." Icicles hung on the ends of his words.

"I know."

"What are you doing here?"

"Isn't it obvious?"

If she didn't stop looking at him with those seductive eyes, he'd... He had no idea what the hell he'd do, but it *couldn't* involve throwing her over his shoulder and carrying her into the house.

"Stay back." He put his hand up to warn her off as he backed away slowly toward his front porch.

"What are you afraid of, Quentin?"

He didn't respond. She knew what she was doing to him. She had turned it into a game.

He was doomed.

"Look, I don't need your mind games. If you forgot something here, I'll ship it to you."

"I didn't forget something, but I did make a terrible, terrible decision and left something very important behind."

He lowered his arm. He probably looked like a fool, and it wasn't doing any good, anyway.

She was still coming toward him.

"Quentin, I never should have left. I'm so, so sorry. I was stupid to let my sadness overrule the happiness you fill me with. I didn't know how to deal with the disappointment of not being able to help my mother, but I know I should have leaned on you. Please give me another chance."

Damn it if tears didn't spring to her gorgeous blue eyes. He could see himself in her watery depths, and the image wasn't a good one.

"Don't cry."

"I don't want to. But someone very important told me it's the only way to heal. And I want us to heal. Please."

He closed his eyes and breathed deep, allowing her scent and her presence to go straight to his head.

"Give me one more chance. Please. I know I'm not perfect, and I know I wasn't great to you or to Joey. I'm better now. I'll be better. I'll do better."

His fingers itched to wipe away the tears that slipped down her cheeks. He tried to turn away, but her unsure smile as she wiped her tears away paralyzed him.

"I'm here to stay, Quentin." Her nervous laugh threw him further off-guard. "Whether you accept me now or I have to work the rest of my life to earn your trust—I'm not going anywhere. I'm setting up shop. I'm rejoining the community. I'll give you all the time you need to realize we belong together. To earn your love."

He stared at her, wishing he had some sort of mind reading ability. He had always considered himself to be a good judge of character, but he had been wrong with her. Or had he? He had vowed not to chase after her. He wouldn't willingly serve his heart to her again.

But she came back on her own. To him. With an acknowledgment of wrongdoing. With apologies.

With goddamned tears.

And she was wearing flip-flops. Not running shoes.

She couldn't bolt with flip-flops.

"Please say something." Her voice was no more

than a squeak. Enough to break him.

"How do I know you won't run again? How can I get my hopes up—Joey's hopes up—without knowing for sure that you'll stay?"

He watched as her tongue darted over her lower lip.

"You don't know. And I understand that." Her hand began to rub the spot that housed her heart. "Quentin, I would never hurt you on purpose. I wasn't thinking of how my actions would affect you or Joey. I was so lost in my own pain that I couldn't even fathom what you were going through. You helped me see outside of my pathetic little world."

Savannah closed her eyes, wrapping her arms around herself. He watched her chest and shoulders rise and fall as she struggled to regain control.

He couldn't take it any longer. He had to hold her, to comfort her. He couldn't put her through this emotional torture.

She held her hands in front of her to keep him from pulling her into his arms.

"Wait. I don't want you to feel sorry for me. I did this. I have to make things up to you, to my parents. To this whole town. And I'll do it. I'm done running. I'm staying. I just hope you'll be holding my hand through it all."

The walls he had worked so hard to build over the last week came tumbling down as easily as a precariously balanced wall of Legos.

"Always. I'll be holding your hand for always."

Her smile was more welcome to him than the sun

on the lake. He barely had time to blink before she jumped into his arms and he had no choice but to catch her.

Fireworks went off when they kissed. She wrapped her legs around his waist; clung to his shoulders. His hands ripped feverishly through her hair. The part of him that tried so desperately to forget about her was dying to see her, to touch her, to love her.

How had he ever managed to convince himself that he could be okay without her?

He turned to carry her up the porch. There would be no more talking. No more arguing. No more fantasizing about ways to hurt her back.

There would only be happiness and damned hot sex from here on out.

"Wait," Savannah mumbled against his lips. "Rocco's in the car."

"He can wait." Quentin growled and nibbled on her neck.

"Too hot." She panted for air, all the while grinding herself against him.

"Get into my bed. I'll let him out."

"Yes, sir."

He let Rocco out of the car and swore under his breath when Nana Robby pulled into the driveway.

His erection may have fled as soon as he knew his son was home, but the eagerness would be around for a long, long time.

***

Not Over You

After a lunch of mac and cheese, chicken nuggets, and fruit, and a giddy reunion with Joey, Savannah couldn't stop smiling. Nana Robby had been a bit frosty with her, but Savannah couldn't blame her after what she had done. She hoped she'd win over the older woman eventually, because she mattered to Savannah's favorite boys. And Savannah intended to spend every minute of the rest of her life trying to be worthy of the Elliot boys.

"Time for graduation! Right, Dad? The clock is on the one!"

Savannah's muscles tightened involuntarily. Yes, graduation was today. Everyone in town liked to gather for the event when the weather was nice enough to hold the ceremony outside in the common.

For the first time today, Savannah silently cursed the sunshine and warmth.

"Yes, Monkey Man. Wash your hands and face, get your shoes on, and I'll race you to the car."

Joey took off like a rock in a slingshot.

Quentin pulled Savannah into his arms, kissed her nose, and asked her to go with them.

She started to say she couldn't, but how could she fully heal if she didn't celebrate this day? She had known many of the kids who were graduating. Her parents would be there—her stepdad had sent her an email invitation to attend, which she had ignored.

"There's going to be a special dedication to Brandon, Savannah," Quentin said. "You should be there."

The now-familiar sting of potential tears pricked the back of her eyes. A dedication. After ten years, they still remembered her brother. They wanted to honor him.

She looked into Quentin's eyes. Their chocolate-swirled depths held a warmth and a familiarity that helped to steady the rapid fluttering of her heart.

"Of course I'll go." A tight knot swelled up from her gut, slowly creeping into her throat. She swallowed hard, trying to suppress it. Grief had kept her paralyzed for far too long. She could feel Brandon here in this town. He deserved to have his moment at graduation.

Quentin hugged her and kissed her on the top of her head. Joey soon rushed through the room, slipped into his sneakers, and shouted, "I'm gonna beat you!"

"Sorry, but I can't lose to a six-year-old."

Savannah laughed at the little boy glint in Quentin's eyes as he turned away from her. He didn't let go of her hand, though. She didn't recognize the giggles coming from her throat as he dragged her out the front door, leaving messy dishes on the counter.

With the exception of the time it took to buckle Joey and settle Rocco into the back seat, Quentin didn't remove his hand from Savannah's the entire way to town.

And even though her palm was sweating and her fingers grew a bit tired and cramped, she didn't try to pull away.

***

Not Over You

The graduation gathering turned into one giant reunion. Everyone she had ever known in town seemed to be fighting their way toward her. Didn't take much to become a celebrity in this town, apparently.

Savannah's mother was still, well, her mother, but they did exchange kisses on the cheek.

"That's what you're wearing to your brother's graduation?"

Savannah felt herself blushing.

"I didn't think about it."

"Of course you didn't." Her mother then dissolved into a coughing fit, so Savannah rushed around to find her a drink of water, then rubbed her back until she regained her breath.

Savannah's stepdad beamed like a lighthouse beacon when the president of the senior class showed him the buttons all of the students were wearing on their graduation robes. Brandon's smiling face would walk down the aisle with each and every student there.

"Do you have your speech prepared, Quentin?" Savannah's mother's voice was almost charming, though still kind of cold, when she questioned Quentin.

Savannah turned to Quentin. "Speech?"

"Yeah, I may have forgotten to mention that." His smile lit up his face. "I was kind of hoping you might want to share some words with the graduating class, too. Since he was your brother and all."

"No. Absolutely not." The temptation to run was strong. *Be stronger, Savannah.* "Why are you giving a speech?"

Her mother interjected. Savannah resisted the urge to tell her to back off and let them have their conversation. "He's giving a speech because he is single-handedly responsible for the gift he's unveiling for the town. In Brandon's name."

"What's the gift?"

Before he could answer, Savannah looked over to the canvas-draped monstrosity. Cranes stood next to the thing, presumably preparing to unveil whatever was underneath.

Quentin leaned down to whisper in her ear, "It's a surprise."

"Come on!"

"Nope. Not telling. The only ones who know are the people who built it, a few select members of the town's planning committee, and your mother. Your dad doesn't even know." The twinkle in his mischievous eyes made her smile, even though she really didn't want to. "I think Joey has some suspicions, but he gave up guessing a while ago, so I haven't had to lie to him or swear him to secrecy. His attention span is still that of a talking teddy bear."

"The ceremony will be starting in five minutes. Let's go find our seats." Savannah's dad began to push her mom down the aisle toward their special seats of honor. Savannah fought tears at the kind gesture of the graduation planning committee. Gratitude warmed her heart.

"Come sit up there with me." Quentin gestured to the stage where other speakers were seated.

She dug in her heels.

Not Over You

"No. Look at me! I'm not dressed for it. And I have nothing of value to say. I barely even graduated from high school. Didn't go to college. I'm not someone who should be spouting off advice."

"Wait one second." Quentin dashed off, returning a minute later with a package. "Here. This is for you."

She removed the graduation robe from the plastic. Full of wrinkles and kind of smelly. She smiled at the insanity of the situation. "I can't wear this."

"Yes you can. For your brother."

How could she say no to that?

She put the wrinkly garment on. Quentin affixed the cap to her head. She pushed her shoulders back, proud to live this moment for her brother.

And admittedly, for her, too.

In a trance of elation, she allowed Quentin to lead her up to the stage. She had never noticed how he could command the space so effectively, but when he introduced her to the superintendent and explained why she was there, she marveled at the respect everyone directed toward Quentin.

All of these official-looking people were on a first name basis with him.

The man could be mayor if he wanted to be. And yet he managed to make her feel like the honored guest.

He led her to her seat, squeezed her shoulders, then sat beside her. When her leg wouldn't stop bouncing, he stilled it with an encouraging and discreet touch. His smile settled her nerves. And when he pulled a jewelry box out of his pocket and handed it to her, she didn't know how to respond.

"I got this for you, but when you weren't going to be here, I figured I'd give it to your mother. But now I want you to have it, and I'll get another one for her later."

Savannah opened the box and gasped at the gorgeous engraved portrait of her brother, set in a platinum setting with mini baseball-styled jewels framing the picture. The portrait was the same one on the sign at the mud park.

She had no words. Luckily for her, someone important (whose name and role she had already forgotten) began speaking into the microphone. Quentin fastened the necklace around her neck. She shivered when his knuckles grazed her sensitive skin. Later. Oh boy, she couldn't wait until later. When she could get him alone.

She strongly suspected that he was responsible for the memorial at Brandon's favorite play place. And now he had created something amazing on the town common.

Getting the approval for whatever it was couldn't have been easy. The people of Healing Springs were notoriously anti-anything-new. They were willing to cater to tourists to keep a healthy economy, and they always voted to fund their schools and libraries, but Savannah clearly remembered a multi-year battle when some citizens wanted to make the town common pond available for ice skating in the winter. And when they wanted to add a little hut for selling snacks and hot cocoa to benefit local sports? Oh, the

Not Over You

war that had ensued!

She tuned into the speech being recited by the woman at the podium when she heard Quentin's name being called. He squeezed her hand before strolling confidently across the stage. Savannah scanned the audience to see who was whistling at her man. The search was futile—too many whistles and hoots and a thunderous applause for her to track down any particularly lusty ladies.

He turned to her and winked before he began to speak.

She had nothing to worry about.

But damn, did these people love him!

Pride forced her to sit upright in her chair. Quentin had come a long way from the poor, neglected child of two not-great, alcoholic and drug-abusing parents. People had looked down upon him all his life. And now he stood in front of an adoring crowd, gifting them with something amazing. Something she was suddenly on the edge of her seat to hear.

He had worked hard to build a financial foundation that would enable him to have the career of his heart—a low-paying profession as a paramedic—while still providing for his family and community.

"Are we ready to see what's behind that canvas wall? I've heard rumors around town—you know who you are—that people are tired of looking at this construction site. Well let's see if this gift from the Brandon Grace Memorial Fund and this year's senior class looks better to all of you gossips out there. I hope to hear some nice rumors about it."

The audience laughed and pointed fingers at one another in jest.

With a wave from Quentin, the cranes lowered the canvas.

The town let out a collective gasp and Savannah cried out in surprise. She clapped her hands over her mouth, sure the entire town was looking at her.

But no, of course they wouldn't be.

Not when all eyes were drawn to the most amazing tree house she had ever seen in her life.

And it was an exact larger-than-life replica of the one Brandon had been building with his Legos when he died.

The town cheered. She leapt out of her seat and threw herself into Quentin's startled arms, not caring a bit about the impropriety of it all.

"Thank you." Her whisper was met with a tightening embrace.

When Savannah finally became aware of where they were and what this day was about, she pulled away and swiped at the wrinkles of her robe, mortified at her public show of affection and gratitude.

Daring to scan the audience, she noticed more than one person dabbing at their eyes or blowing noses.

Everyone loved Brandon. Even in his death, he represented the heart and soul of this town.

The band struck up a cheerful tune. Savannah inched her way toward her seat, but was stopped by the sudden silence of the band and Quentin's voice over the stage speakers.

Not Over You

"Please welcome Savannah Grace to deliver some words of memorial. Savannah?"

Her feet tried to drill holes in the plywood stage. Her eyes threatened to deliver great harm to Quentin. But as he stood there before the entire town, beaming with pride, her anger and fear dissolved.

She stepped forward, completely unprepared, but eager to have this moment for Brandon.

"Thank you, friends and family, for giving me this opportunity." Her voice squeaked. Someone from the back of the audience shouted out for her to speak into the microphone. She cleared her throat.

"Better?" A loud, high-pitched squeal from the microphone had everyone complaining and covering their ears. She looked helplessly at Quentin, who came over and adjusted it for her, then set her at ease with a smile.

"Let's hope the third time is a charm." Savannah's voice sounded ridiculously loud to her own ears, but the vocal members of the audience gave her a thumbs-up.

"I'm thrilled to be here in the town that Brandon loved so much. Most of you had the privilege to know him. But for those of you who are new to town, you really missed out on one of the best souls you'd ever meet. If you asked Brandon what he would do when he grew up, he'd probably tell you something like, 'I want to build tree houses for the children of Healing Springs.' That's the kind of kid he was. And that's the dream that you brought to fruition here today."

Savannah lowered her head, summoning the

memory of Brandon's smile to give her strength. She cleared her throat and continued.

"Graduates, your life isn't just beginning—it's been happening all along. Brandon would have walked this very stage today if not for a terrible tragedy."

She cleared her throat again. *You can do this, Savannah Grace.*

"Thankfully, Brandon was the kind of kid who always lived as if the day was a gift to him. I wasn't here to say goodbye to Brandon. Now I realize I don't have to. He lives on in every one of us. In every one of you. In the very air we breathe. We may not see him, but he is here. He is in every kind word you share with a friend. He is in every hug, every handshake. His silly laughter carries on the breeze even now. Can you feel him?"

Tears pooled in Savannah's eyes when a student in the second row raised her hand up to the sky, head back, eyes closed. The entire student body followed suit. A giant breeze blew, knocking unsecured hats off of heads and forcing a collective, "ooh," out of the audience.

"See? He was always a trickster."

The audience laughed and fixed their caps.

"You may think that I, as the big sister, did most of the teaching. I thought so, too. But boy was I wrong. What could I possibly have learned from an eight-year-old boy? I don't have time to tell you everything. I know you're all eager to get those diplomas and toss those caps in the air. But in honor of Brandon, I want to share a few things I've learned that I think can carry

Not Over You

you all a long way on your journey.

"First of all, always pitch the baseball one more time. The person at the bat might just need one more chance.

"When someone you love is in a terrible mood, tell them the worst joke you can think of. They'll laugh. Even ten years later.

"And finally, but most importantly, show the ones you love that you love them every single chance you get. This is one I'm still working on. It can be hard. Life can be painful. But living without the ones you love the most and always wondering if they knew what they meant to you is the worst kind of pain in the world. Don't let yourself find this out the hard way."

The only sound to pierce through the silence was the sound of sniffling and crinkling tissues.

Damn, this was a celebration and she had managed to depress everyone. She should have led with the hard stuff and left off with the advice about the jokes.

She took a deep breath.

"Thank you to everyone in Healing Springs, especially Quentin Elliot, for this amazing donation. Brandon would have given his approval. And even though you're all graduating and thinking you're all grown up, I expect to see you playing in that remarkable structure as often as you possibly can. Life is too short not to play!"

Applause swelled through the crowd. People started rising to their feet, groups at a time, until the entire audience—give or take a few elderly members—

were delivering a standing ovation that she didn't feel she deserved.

She looked to Quentin, whose teary eyes matched hers. He clapped harder than the rest.

He was the one who deserved the praise. Not her.

He walked toward her, clapping the entire way. He held his arm out and began to lead her back to her seat.

"Not so fast." The principal of the high school spoke into the microphone. "Savannah, please come back here."

She did as told.

"I wasn't here ten years ago, but as I understand it, we have something that belongs to you."

Savannah swore her heart had vacated her body. She couldn't even take a breath. What was this?

An older gentleman stepped forward, and when he got closer, she recognized him as her history teacher. One of her favorites. He held out two diplomas and a hand for a handshake.

She didn't know what to say.

"One for you, one for your brother."

She held the diplomas tight to her chest, feeling the burn of love deep within.

"Thank you. So much."

She stood like an idiot until Quentin came to her rescue, escorting her back to her seat like the gentleman he was.

Savannah continued to clutch the diplomas to her chest throughout the rest of the ceremony, grinning like a fool.

Not Over You

When everything was over and people were gathering together, Quentin pulled her to a hidden spot behind the stage.

"I've been dying to get you alone." His husky voice made every part of her tremble in a very needy way.

"We're not exactly alone."

"Close enough." His lips lingered over hers for a torturous moment. His hands, warm and strong on her lower back, made her arch into him.

"I feel so naughty here. Just like the old days."

"Yeah, we did do this a time or two, didn't we?" He pulled her even closer, making the diplomas cut into her belly.

"Sneak away to make out? Um, yeah. All the time. Pretty sure I'm still grounded according to my mother and her threats of 'indefinite grounding.'"

"Can we not talk about your mother right now?" Quentin growled.

"I think that's exactly what we need to talk about. Because I'm sure they're all looking for us. Especially since you left Joey sitting with them."

His forehead bumped hers as he groaned in frustration.

"Fine, but later—you'd better be ready for me."

That was a threat she could live with.

"Always."

He stepped away from her in order to regain his composure before clutching her hand and leading her into the fray.

Savannah thought her face would crack under the intensity of her smile when Joey grabbed her hand and led her toward the tree house. The little bundle of energy had as much confidence as his father did. Tossing her hair over her shoulder, she smiled even more when she noticed Quentin pushing her mother's wheelchair.

"Joseph Brandon, you wait up, young man!" Savannah's mother sounded stronger than she had lately.

Savannah turned toward Quentin, raising her brows in question. He had given his son her brother's name?

He nodded and blew a kiss.

She smiled, feeling more at peace than ever before.

Serenity made her mother's face softer, more approachable. Kinder. Her dad walked with lighter steps, grinning widely as he studied both diplomas as he walked.

"Wow, you thought of everything!" Savannah marveled at the design of the tree house. Not only was there a fabulous set of steps with rope handles, but a ramp spiraled around the tree as well, wide enough for a wheelchair.

"Brandon was always inclusive of everyone, right? He didn't see differences in people. He hadn't designed a wheelchair accessible entrance yet, but I know he would have eventually. He'd want all kids to have the ability to enjoy this beast of a tree house."

Savannah's mother reached up to stroke Quentin's arm. After all the trouble she had given Savannah all those years ago about dating the town "riff raff,"

Not Over You

Savannah could hardly believe that they had formed this close relationship.
Miracles truly could occur.
And she got to live in the midst of them.

Chapter Sixteen

Cuddling into Quentin's sweaty skin, Savannah suddenly remembered the things she wanted to tell him.

Every time she started to speak, he changed the subject in such a delicious way, she lost track of her thoughts again.

Joey was having a sleepover at Savannah's parent's house—her mother had insisted. Savannah had almost fainted from the shock, but Quentin had hinted that this wasn't the first time. Apparently her mother had developed a soft spot for little Joey.

Nana Robby made a point of saying she would be visiting a friend at Hampton Beach for the rest of the weekend, so they had the entire house to themselves.

They even locked Rocco in the other room with a giant treat ball stuffed with peanut butter. No disruptions.

Savannah couldn't remember the last time her body tingled so much. Her skin had become so sensitive that the tiniest movement or slightest rush of air had her shivering in delight.

"You had something you wanted to say?" Quentin looked up at her as he nuzzled her belly button.

"Yes, but you need to get up here."

He obliged, capturing her lips and stroking her in *other places*.

Mustering every bit of strength she possessed, she pushed him away.

His pout was perfect. To soothe his wounded pride, she flipped over and leaned on his chest. She kissed his chin, then his ear.

"You're my defibrillator, you know."

"I'd argue that you're mine. You certainly know how to shock my heart."

"You're the healer. You helped me heal. You help others heal. I just need to make sure you understand something."

He pushed himself up so he was leaning against the backboard, suddenly serious.

"What's the matter, Peaches?"

"As much as you feel the need to heal people, I need you to know that I'm okay. I do need your love, but I don't need you to fix me." She shifted away from him slightly, half-expecting him to be offended.

"What's there to fix?" He put his arm over her shoulders and pulled her to him. "You're the strongest person I've ever met in my entire life. You are my inspiration for wanting to heal people. Not because I need to fix you, but because I want to help. Just like you help everyone you meet. Don't grunt at me. You think you're such a loner, but you don't see the trail you leave behind. Everyone who has ever had any contact with you is left feeling uplifted, even when you have suffered."

"So not true."

"You want to argue about it?"

"No."

She settled into his embrace, turning so she could play with his light chest hair.

"I have something else to tell you," she whispered.

"You'd better not be confessing that you're secretly married or something."

"Not unless you drugged me and dragged me to Vegas."

"Hmm, why didn't I think of that?"

She slapped him playfully.

"I wanted to let you know that I'll be donating bone marrow."

"Was there an error with the test results? That's great, Peaches!"

"No error. I'll be donating to a ten-year-old girl somewhere out west."

"That's amazing! You're amazing." Quentin's arms cradled her. She had never looked for comfort from a man in the last decade—only physical release. She couldn't believe how easily she had learned to enjoy his touch again. She hoped she'd marvel every day for the rest of her life.

"The people at the donor bank said it's really unusual to match so quickly."

"They're telling the truth."

"I guess it helps me to feel like I'm doing

something good."

"Peaches, this is meant to be. You intended to donate to your mother. She has already found another match. And now you have matched with someone, too? Incredibly rare. Definitely meant to be." He cupped her chin and lifted her face toward his. "This is your chance to forgive yourself. Miss Molly would say that Healing Springs struck again."

"I don't know about that, but something in this town has definitely made my life better."

"The fresh air?"

"Yeah, that too."

"The irresistible men?"

"One of them, anyway."

"The hot sex?"

"Hmm, have I had any of that yet?"

He lifted her leg so she'd straddle him and slapped her ass.

"Guess I'll have to remind you."

"Promise?"

"On one condition."

"There are conditions to getting an orgasm? What kind of agreement have I entered here?"

"I think you'll find the terms favorable. I hope so, anyway. You only have to swear to love me forever. To be my partner in crime. To let me try my hardest to keep that gorgeous smile on that beautiful face."

"Is that a proposal?" she joked. His face turned even more serious. "I was kidding."

"I wasn't."

She looked away.

"I'm not saying you should marry me this minute—though if you wanted to, I wouldn't say no. But I intend to marry you. Soon."

"Quentin—"

"Shh. You know you want to."

"I do. It's just—"

"There's nothing to say after 'I do.'"

"I don't know if I can give you what you need or want."

"You already do."

Tears spilled out even though she squeezed her eyes tight.

Quentin wiped away her tears with his two big thumbs. His gentle voice soothed her in unimaginable ways.

"If you decide you want children, great. I'll be on board. If not, I just ask that you love Joey like he's your own. Your life doesn't have to change at all—you just have to share it with me."

"I do love him, Quentin. I love him so much. He has completely captured my heart. He glued together fragments that I thought had long ago disintegrated."

"He's good like that."

"He's just like *you* like that."

Quentin kissed her again, exactly like she wanted him to. The sneaky devil slipped himself inside her, too, and she wasn't surprised to realize her body was fully ready and accepting of his intrusion.

"Actually," he muttered against her lips. "I have to amend what I said. You do have to change one thing."

She stiffened, and then groaned. She really

wanted to move against him, but she had to pay attention to what he was saying.

"As the love of my life, I fully disapprove of your bar habits. If you'd like to dress up in stilettos and tight clothes, it should be me you're seducing."

She laughed out loud, relieved that he was playing.

"I'm not kidding."

"As long as you're a good boy, you'll have nothing to worry about."

"Oh, I'll be good," he growled. And then he rolled her over, pinned her hands above her head, and showed her just how good he could be.

***

Savannah shook her head and gestured for Quentin to move the picture over to the left. When he had it perfectly lined up, she smiled and admired their work. The framed photo collage of Joey and Rocco playing was the perfect decoration for her brand new gourmet dog food store, scheduled to open in less than a week.

"Hey, I know I promised I wouldn't mention it again for a while, but it has been a few months and we haven't finished the paperwork." Quentin pulled her in for a hip-to-hip hug—the kind she liked the best. He kissed her forehead, then her cheeks, then teased the corners of her lips before delivering the kiss she needed from him.

"Are we sure?" She searched his face for clues. Did

he really believe she could do this?

"I thought so, but if you're not ready..."

"I am. I've waited long enough to give back to the world. There are so many kids who need homes, and you have that giant house just begging to be filled."

He kissed her again.

"We could do the dog rescue instead, if you want."

"And risk the wrath of Joey? He's been begging for a sibling. And I love the idea of taking in foster kids."

"Then it's settled." Quentin stared in her eyes. She'd never get tired of this shared intimacy.

"Oh, and I forgot to tell you. I got a call from my lawyer today—Merry withdrew the custody suit. After not showing up for the visit we had arranged, she must have realized it wouldn't go her way." She could hear the relief in his voice; could feel his muscles relax.

"Good! She never should have done that." Savannah hugged him tight. "I still can't believe she didn't show. Good thing you decided not to tell Joey. I just wish things could be different for him. I know he needs his mom."

"Yeah, she has no idea what she's missing. He's a great kid and deserves so much better. Good thing he has better now."

"I could never replace his mom."

"Have you noticed his nightmares have stopped? He didn't know his mother, so he couldn't miss her. He only missed the loving female influence he fantasized about. You have filled that role for him. You are his mother."

"I couldn't be more proud. And no stretch marks!

Easiest delivery ever."

Quentin pinched her butt, making her squeal.

"All right, mister. Back to work. We still have to set up the doggy feeding stations."

"I still can't believe you got this past the Board of Selectman. It was one thing to propose a store where you sell the food, but a drop-in doggy restaurant? Unbelievable."

"I have my charms."

"Oh, I know."

"Come in the kitchen and I'll remind you."

"The kitchen? You naughty girl."

"It's just you and me, right? How often does that happen?"

"Not nearly often enough. You locked the door?"

She nodded, biting her bottom lip in what she hoped was a seductive manner. He lifted her up, carried her to the kitchen, and showed her the best use for a stainless steel counter.

Amanda Torrey

Stay: Chapter One

"If you turn down the dare, your picture goes up on the wall."

Ava O'Connor tensed at the thought of her supposed-to-be-innocent kindergarten-teacher face being plastered to the Wall of Shame for all to see.

"Jake, you'd make an exception for me, wouldn't you?" Ava did her best to smile sweetly, but she had a feeling she looked more like she had swallowed something sour. Like her pride.

"Sorry, kitten." The bartender didn't look sorry. In fact, he looked downright pleased. "You know the rules. You enter the closet for three minutes and everyone gets a free round of drinks, or you decline the dare and you live on my wall for eternity."

"Not fair." The urge to stomp her foot in protest welled within her, but she stopped herself before her inner child came tearing through the room. Not even inner children belonged in bars.

"Karly, I swear I'll kill you." Ava glared at her so-called best friend. "It's bad enough you know I can't turn down a dare, but knowing that I couldn't allow my face to be on that wall even if I *could* say no... Shame on you."

"Just get your ass in there and I won't pick out the nastiest guy in the room."

"Make sure he's a non-smoker. I do *not* want to kiss an ashtray."

"Suddenly you have high standards."

Ava tossed a Jake's Lounge coaster at Karly.

"You're a terrible best friend."

"You won't say that when your three minutes in Heaven are up. Now go. The lights are flashing. I have to find someone willing to kiss your prudish face." Karly shoved Ava toward the neon-framed door. "Come on, this is better than getting married. Get going."

Karly slapped Ava's butt as Ava dragged herself toward the door. Why had she deviated from her normal Friday night routine of ice cream on her couch with a chick flick and her dog for company? She had made it this far into her twenties without having to endure this humiliation.

So much for best friends having your best interests at heart. Karly had sworn this would help Ava get over the sting of being dumped so terribly by her fiancé. Karly felt it was the perfect night to go out, since this was the day Ava was supposed to get married.

Okay, after six months maybe she did need to rejoin society.

But not like this.

Ava closed the door behind her and began to panic. She hadn't even grabbed a mint!

Heat burned her cheeks.

She puffed into her closed hands to see how badly her breath smelled. The faint scent of rum and Coke reassured her—at least she hadn't had the blooming onion appetizer yet.

Three minutes. How bad could it be? There had been plenty of decent-looking guys in the bustling Friday night crowd. Surely Karly would choose well.

Not that it mattered to her what the guy looked like. She judged men on more than their surface appearance. Besides, she wasn't *breeding* with the guy. Just a kiss. An anonymous, one-time, never-to-be-spoken-of-again moment of mortification.

Ava's throat began to close as a horrifying thought crippled her ability to breathe.

What if a student's dad was chosen?

She'd have to resign!

She'd have to move!

She'd have to go into the witness protection program!

The door opened and closed before she could escape. She wiped her sweaty hands on her jeans. The air thickened as the guy settled into the small space.

He didn't smell unpleasant, she supposed. In fact, there was something dangerously familiar about his particular fragrance. A woodshop—that's what it was. He smelled like wood. And the clean smell of someone who had recently showered.

A strict no talking rule applied, which felt incredibly awkward. Ava's belly clenched. Was she supposed to just reach up and feel until she found his

Not Over You

lips? Or was he supposed to make the first move?

She didn't want to mess up this dare. Any missteps and she'd be on the Wall of Shame. And this mystery guy—now that the challenge had been accepted—would be on the wall alongside her. Everyone in Healing Springs would know that they had been in this closet together. Generations of people would gawk at them.

Unable to endure the apprehension any longer, Ava leaned forward for a kiss. She kissed his chest.

Super.

His rough-textured hand found her chin and positioned her face. Her body stirred. This was way too familiar for her taste. She had to get this over with before any more memories surfaced. Her history with men was deplorable—she had no need to relive any of it.

Mystery man's lips touched hers, and something zinged inside her. The kiss took on a life of its own. She lost control and began clinging to his arms like her life depended on it.

The loss of control was mutual. Their tongues met and danced and she knew without a doubt that the mystery man was no mystery. The only mystery, in fact, was why the hell he was in town.

***

The second the buzzer went off, Ava pushed Cole out of the way and stumbled out of the dark. The normally dim lights of the bar mocked her with their brightness as her pupils adjusted. Her heart thundered, making her wish she could rip it out and fling it at Karly.

"Whoa, slow down, sista." Karly reached out to steady Ava. "Bad kisser?"

"The worst," Ava lied, her chest rising and falling with each angry breath she took. "Why him?"

"I saw him checking you out earlier. And he's fucking hot. Figured he'd be the perfect reintroduction to the world of *lust*."

"It was a terrible idea."

"Damn. Never would have guessed. Hell, if he hadn't been ogling you from across the room, I would have been on him like an ant on a picnic lunch."

The thought of Karly moving in on Cole made her even more angry, though she had no right to be.

"He didn't try anything naughty, did he? That's against the rules."

"No, just a kiss."

Calming down, Ava was able to hear the rowdy yahoos as the round of drinks were served. Random people kept patting her on the back. She didn't dare to turn around. She couldn't chance seeing Cole again.

"I'm done." Ava slumped into her stool, burying her head on her shaking arms. She turned to look through her wavy hair at Karly, who rubbed her shoulders in empathy that was coming too late.

"I'm proud of you for giving it a try. Next time I'll pick a better one."

Ava shot up in her seat. "There will not be a next time."

Karly threw her hands up in surrender. "Okay,

okay! No more dares. But give me another chance, will you? I can do better. Maybe that guy over there."

Against her better judgment, Ava looked.

"Way too young. And way too male. Come on, I did as you asked. Can't I please go home now?"

"One dance, and then we'll leave. Even though I haven't even scored a free drink yet." Karly pouted. "This is how I shall sacrifice for you."

Karly's lips lifted in the corner as she raised her eyebrows for effect.

"I'll buy you a drink," Ava offered.

"Yeah, but will you put out after?" Karly laughed as Ava rolled her eyes. "Didn't think so."

"And hey, I went into the closet so you could have a stinking free drink. Where's your gratitude?"

"You know what I mean." Karly looked past Ava, searching the crowd. "It's not a night out if at least one hottie doesn't buy me a drink."

Ava leaned toward Karly so she wouldn't have to shout.

"Do you still see him here? Or did he leave?"

"I haven't seen him—was caught up with you. Didn't even see him leave the closet. Want me to go find him and see if the second time is better?"

"No!"

"I was kidding. Loosen the girdle, Mildred."

Karly's gaze drifted over Ava's shoulder. Ava knew Karly had spotted a potential target by the way she pulled the front of her shirt down a bit before readjusting her low-cut jeans.

"If you'll excuse me, my bartender has returned

from his break."

"Your boobs are about to fall out of your shirt."

Karly winked and smiled saucily.

"Let's hope so."

"What about the dance?" Ava's question ended in a whisper as Karly moved toward the end of the bar, intent upon catching the guy before any of the other desirables made their move.

She rested her head in her hand as she surveyed the area. Cole wasn't seated at the bar, and she didn't dare look into the club section. A group of out-of-place businessmen who looked to be in their forties stopped talking to stare her way. She quickly broke eye contact, not wanting to send the wrong message. All the women she had seen so far were heavily made up as if vying for a role. Most sexy? Ava knew she'd lose. Most beautiful? Yup, not a chance. Most fun? Ha. She'd put old Mrs. Reynolds to sleep. Most lame? Now that was a title she had a chance of securing.

Karly leaned over the bar, showing her attributes to the bartender as they flirted. How could seduction come so easily to some? Ava would never feel comfortable behaving that way. And her chest wasn't ample enough to do the talking.

She blew a curl out of her face. Not accustomed to drinking, the alcohol seemed to be hitting Ava faster than she anticipated. Especially her bladder.

If Karly was still busy with her prey when Ava returned from the bathroom, she'd take it as a sign that she was free to go home.

For a small town, Jake's Lounge sure attracted a

crowd on a Friday night. She shoved her way through, annoyed that no one would just *move politely.*

She had to pass that blasted closet to get to the bathroom. The visual reminder was too much—her body started warring with her brain.

Four years had passed since she had last been with Cole. Four years. So why did her body react to him as if he had never left at all? As if he had never stomped on her heart with his steel-toed work boots?

She didn't mean to seek him out, but there he was. Bent over the pool table, ready to take a shot. His perfect butt called out to her—would he notice if she squeezed it?

Ava mentally slapped herself.

Get to the bathroom and get out of here.

But her body had different ideas. *Just a few steps. Toss him on the pool table. No one will notice. Or blame you.*

She actually took a step in his direction before her head kindly interrupted. *He's a creep! A womanizer! Walk away! Listen to me. I won't let you down again.*

But he's so ungodly hot! Her body refused to give any control to her head.

A slender arm—not hers—wrapped itself around her fantasy man's arm. Ava glared at the sexy woman staring adoringly up at Cole. The man who had only moments ago given Ava the best kiss she had had in, well, four years.

Ava narrowed her eyes and wished one of the fluttering-eyed woman's fake eyelashes would fall off, then shook her head to clear it of mean thoughts.

Mean thoughts were not very kindergarten-teacher-like!

Cole smiled at the woman, and even from across the room, Ava was taunted by the crater-deep dimple that taunted her like a steak dangling before a dog.

She hadn't realized she had been staring until Cole made eye contact with her.

Ava gasped, feeling like one of her kindergartner's getting caught dumping soap all over the bathroom floor. Embarrassment and shame made her walk faster across the bar.

Time to get out of here. While she still had a tiny bit of her pride.

A hand grasping her arm stopped her from continuing her frenzied flight from the bar.

She whipped around, ready to do battle. She wished she had pepper spray or something. Anything to keep him from hurting her.

Not physically, of course.

But wasn't emotional pain just as bad?

"Ava—it's so good to see you in the light." His voice washed over her like bubbles in a Jacuzzi tub. Soothing, gentle, warm. A welcoming smile graced his face. As if they should be happy to see each other. As if he had never broken her heart.

"Sorry, I was just leaving."

"Come on. I haven't seen you in years. Don't rush off."

"You were a little preoccupied. I think she's looking for you now, matter-of-fact." Ava tried to pull away, but he grabbed her other arm and twisted her body toward his. Someone in the crowd bumped against her, pushing her dangerously close to his hard body.

"I don't even know her."

"That's reassuring." Ava rolled her eyes. *Men.*

"I wasn't with her, if that's what you're thinking. She just started coming on to me. There's only one woman here who interests me."

Cole's eyes drifted to her lips, and she caught herself licking them before pulling the lower portion in for a bite.

This wasn't her game. She had no idea how to play it.

He leaned down. He was going to kiss her. He was *so* going to kiss her. Shouldn't she pull away? Shouldn't she stomp on his foot? Shouldn't she—

What was she trying to tell herself?

All she could focus on was the dark scruff on his face and his ridiculously long lashes as his eyes drifted closed and he prepared to strike.

He pulled her body closer. Her hips wiggled to find a good landing spot, even against her better judgment.

Ah, to hell with judgment.

His lips joined hers with as much passion as she had imagined. She lost herself in him.

She heard an animal growling, or maybe it was her. She needed to break away. She needed to run away. Danger! Danger!

She kissed deeper.

Thankfully, he pulled away. She had no control over her teeth grabbing his lower lip and refusing to let go.

What the heck?

His hand cupped her cheek with too much tenderness and familiarity. He wasn't some stranger she had picked up in the bar. He was the man she had hooked up with for an entire summer and then was left behind with barely a goodbye.

And even knowing that, she still wanted to push him against the bar, climb up on a stool, and unleash the endowment he kept hidden behind that burgeoning zipper.

"Come with me, Ava. My place is right down the street from here."

Of course he did. And of course he came here tonight with the intention of scoring. Isn't that what everyone was after?

Not her. Definitely not with him.

"How convenient for you," she spat, finally able to pull away and mean it.

His puzzled expression was nearly her undoing. How dare he look confused?

She turned on her heel, pushed her way through the crowd, and stormed out the door, not even caring that she didn't tell Karly she was leaving.

More From Amanda Torrey

If you enjoyed this book, would you please consider leaving an honest review where you purchased the book? Reviews help other readers discover new authors and help authors be able to write more books. The review doesn't have to be lengthy—even a couple of sentences would be great! Thank you so much for being the best reader ever.

To be notified of future releases, and to be eligible to win "subscriber only" prizes, please sign up for Amanda's newsletter. You can sign up on Amanda's website. Amanda loves to hear from readers, so please find her online!

Books by Amanda Torrey

Teen Fury Trilogy (Young Adult Paranormal)
    Unleashed (Book One)
    Embraced (Book Two)
    Atoned (Book Three)
    Teen Fury Trilogy: The Complete Collection (Boxed Set)

Healing Springs Series (Adult Contemporary Romance)
Books in this series can be read in any order
    Not Over You
    Stay
    A Heart to Call Home
    Two Is A Lonely Number
    Loving a Wildflower
    So Complicated
    Wherever You Go

Also by Amanda Torrey

The Immortal Contract (Adult Paranormal Romance)

Made in the USA
Middletown, DE
10 October 2020